THE LEGEND
OF SLEEPY HOLLOW

THE LEGEND
OF SLEEPY HOLLOW
BY WASHINGTON IRVING

ILLUSTRATED BY
ARTHUR RACKHAM

ILLUSTRATED
STORIES
FOR CHILDREN

DERRYDALE

New York

This 1998 edition is published by Derrydale,
a division of Random House Value Publishing, Inc.,
201 East 50th Street, New York, New York 10022.

Derrydale® is a registered trademark of
Random House Value Publishing, Inc.

Random House
New York • Toronto • London • Sydney • Auckland
http://www.randomhouse.com/

Printed and bound in Singapore

Library of Congress Cataloging-in-Publication Data
Irving, Washington, 1783-1859.
     The legend of Sleepy Hollow / by Washington Irving ; illustrated by
Arthur Rackham.
          p.   cm. — (Illustrated stories for children)
     Summary: A superstitious schoolmaster, in love with a wealthy
farmer's daughter, has a terrifying encounter with a headless horseman.
     ISBN 0-517-20303-0
     [1. Ghosts—Fiction. 2. New York (State)—Fiction.] I. Rackham,
Arthur, 1867-1939, ill. II. Title. III. Series.
PZ7.I68Le 1998
[Fic]—dc21   97-51194
                                                                            CIP
                                                                             AC

8 7 6 5 4 3 2

*Illustration on page 93 by Rustyn L. Birch,
based on a painting by Arthur Rackham*

Introduction

Welcome to Sleepy Hollow, a quiet little village near the eastern shore of the Hudson River. Here descendants from the original Dutch settlers live in peace and harmony, only occasionally disturbed by the ghosts and spirits that they firmly believe haunt this enchanted area.

The spirit who seems to command all the others is a headless horseman, known by some as the Galloping Hessian, who is frequently sighted as he rides through the countryside in search of his head which he lost in battle during the Revolutionary War.

In Sleepy Hollow you will meet Ichobad Crane, the village schoolteacher and singing master, who delights the villagers with his stories of New England witchcraft and dire omens. You will become acquainted with

Katrina van Tassel, the rosy-cheeked young daughter of a wealthy Dutch farmer. And you will certainly be impressed by young Brom van Blunt, known as Brom Bones, who is famous round the countryside for his feats of strength, his expert horsemanship, and his daring adventures.

The Legend of Sleepy Hollow, which is today considered a classic in American literature, was written in 1820 by Washington Irving. Eight-five years later Arthur Rackham, a well-known British artist, did the marvelous illustrations that appear in this book.

Now, come to Sleepy Hollow. Don't be frightened by the ghosts and goblins, fearful shapes and dark shadows, strange sounds and eerie gusts of wind. Enter this pretty village and discover the legend that made it famous.

THE LEGEND
OF SLEEPY HOLLOW
FOUND AMONG THE PAPERS OF THE
LATE DIEDRICH KNICKERBOCKER

A pleasing land of drowsy-head it was,
   Of dreams that wave before the half-shut
     eye,
And of gay castles in the clouds that pass,
   Forever flushing round a summer sky.
CASTLE OF INDOLENCE

In the bosom of one of those spacious coves
which indent the eastern shore of the Hudson,
at that broad expansion of the river denominated by the ancient Dutch navigators

the Tappan Zee, and where they always prudently shortened sail and implored the protection of St. Nicholas when they crossed, there lies a small market town or rural port which by some is called Greensburg, but which is more generally and properly known by the name of Tarry Town. This name was given, we are told, in former days by the good housewives of the adjacent country from the inveterate propensity of their husbands to linger about the village tavern on market days. Be that as it may, I do not vouch for the fact, but merely advert to it for the sake of being precise and authentic.

Not far from this village, perhaps about two miles, there is a little valley, or rather lap of land, among high hills, which is one of the quietest places in the whole world. A small brook glides through it, with just murmur enough to lull one to repose, and the occasional whistle of a quail or tapping of a woodpecker is almost the only sound that ever breaks in upon the uniform tranquility.

I recollect that when a stripling my first exploit in squirrel-shooting was in a grove of tall walnut trees that shades one side of the valley. I had wandered into it at noontime, when all Nature is peculiarly quiet, and was startled by the roar of my own gun as it broke the Sabbath stillness around and was prolonged and reverberated by the angry echoes. If ever I should wish for a retreat whither I might steal from the world and its distractions and dream quietly away the remnant of a troubled life, I know of none more promising than this little valley.

From the listless repose of the place and the peculiar character of its inhabitants, who are descendants from the original Dutch settlers, this sequestered glen has long been known by the name of Sleepy Hollow, and its rustic lads are called the Sleepy Hollow Boys throughout all the neighboring country. A drowsy, dreamy influence seems to hang over the land and to pervade the very atmosphere. Some say that the place was bewitched by a High

German doctor during the early days of the
settlement; others, that an old Indian chief,
the prophet or wizard of his tribe, held his
powwows there before the country was discovered by Master Hendrick Hudson. Certain
it is, the place still continues under the sway of
some witching power that holds a spell over
the minds of the good people, causing them to
walk in a continual reverie. They are given
to all kinds of marvelous beliefs, are subject
to trances and visions, and frequently see
strange sights and hear music and voices in

the air. The whole neighborhood abounds with local tales, haunted spots, and twilight superstitions; stars shoot and meteors glare oftener across the valley than in any other part of the country, and the nightmare, with her whole ninefold, seems to make it the favorite scene of her gambols.

The dominant spirit, however, that haunts this enchanted region, and seems to be commander-in-chief of all the powers of the air, is the apparition of a figure on horseback without a head. It is said by some to be the ghost of a Hessian trooper whose head had

been carried away by a cannonball in some nameless battle during the Revolutionary War, and who is ever and anon seen by the countryfolk hurrying along in the gloom of night as if on the wings of the wind. His haunts are not confined to the valley, but extend at times to the adjacent roads, and especially to the vicinity of a church at no great distance. Indeed, certain of the most authentic historians of those parts, who have been careful in collecting and collating the floating facts concerning this specter, allege that, the body of the trooper having been buried in the churchyard, the ghost rides forth to the scene of battle in nightly quest of his head, and that the rushing speed with which he sometimes passes along the Hollow, like a midnight blast, is owing to his being belated and in a hurry to get back to the churchyard before daybreak.

Such is the general purport of this legendary superstition, which has furnished materials for many a wild story in that region

of shadows; and the specter is known at all the country firesides by the name of the Headless Horseman of Sleepy Hollow.

It is remarkable that the visionary propensity I have mentioned is not confined to native inhabitants of the valley, but is unconsciously imbibed by everyone who resides there for a time. However wide awake they may have been before they entered that sleepy region, they are sure in a little time to inhale the witching influence of the air and begin to grow imaginative—to dream dreams and see apparitions.

I mention this peaceful spot with all possible laud, for it is in such little retired Dutch valleys, found here and there embosomed in the great State of New York, that population, manners, and customs remain fixed, while the

great torrent of migration and improvement, which is making such incessant changes in other parts of this restless country, sweeps by them unobserved. They are like those little nooks of still water which border a rapid stream where we may see the straw and bubble riding quietly at anchor or slowly revolving in their mimic harbor, undisturbed by the rush of the passing current. Though many years have elapsed since I trod the drowsy shades of Sleepy Hollow, yet I question whether I should not still find the same trees and the same families vegetating in its sheltered bosom.

In this by-place of Nature there abode, in a remote period of American history—that is to say, some thirty years since—a worthy wight of the name of Ichabod Crane, who sojourned, or, as he expressed it, "tarried," in Sleepy Hollow for the purpose of instructing the children of the vicinity. He was a native of

Connecticut, a state which supplies the Union with pioneers for the mind as well as for the forest, and sends forth yearly its legions of frontier woodmen and country schoolmasters.

The cognomen of Crane was not inapplicable to his person. He was tall, but exceedingly lank, with narrow shoulders, long arms and legs, hands that dangled a mile out of his sleeves, feet that might have served for shovels, and his whole frame most loosely hung together. His head was small, and flat at top, with huge ears, large green glassy eyes, and a long snipe nose, so that it looked like a weathercock perched upon his spindle neck to tell which way the wind blew. To see him striding along the profile of a hill on a windy day, with his clothes bagging and fluttering about him, one might have mistaken him for the genius of Famine descending upon the earth or some scarecrow eloped from a cornfield.

His schoolhouse was a low building of one

large room, rudely constructed of logs, the windows partly glazed and partly patched with leaves of old copybooks. It was most ingeniously secured at vacant hours by a slender twig twisted in the handle of the door and stakes set against the window shutters, so that, though a thief might get in with perfect ease, he would find some embarrassment in getting out—an idea most probably borrowed by the architect, Yost Van Houten, from the mystery of an eel pot.

The schoolhouse stood in a rather lonely but pleasant situation, just at the foot of a woody hill, with a brook running close by and a formidable birch tree growing at one end of it. From hence the low murmur of his pupils' voices, memorizing their lessons, might be heard on a drowsy summer's day like the hum of a beehive, interrupted now and then by the authoritative voice of the master in the tone of menace or command, or, possibly, by the appalling sound of the birch as he urged some tardy loiterer along the flowery path of knowledge. Truth to say, he was a conscientious man, and always bore in mind the golden maxim, "Spare the rod and spoil the child." Ichabod Crane's scholars certainly were not spoiled.

I would not have it imagined, however, that he was one of those cruel potentates of the school who take joy in the pain of their subjects; on the contrary, he administered justice with discrimination rather than severity, taking the burden off the backs of the weak and laying it on those of the strong. Your mere puny stripling, who winced at the least flourish of the rod, was passed by with indulgence; but the claims of justice were satisfied by inflicting a double portion on some little tough, wrong-headed Dutch urchin, who sulked and swelled and grew dogged and sullen beneath the birch. All this he called "doing his duty by their parents"; and he never inflicted a chastisement without following it by the assurance, so consolatory to the smarting urchin, that "he would remember it and thank him for it the longest day he had to live."

When school hours were over he was even the companion and playmate of the larger

boys, and on holiday afternoons would con-
voy home some of the smaller ones who
happened to have pretty sisters or good housewives for mothers noted for the comforts of
the cupboard. Indeed, it behooved him to
keep on good terms with his pupils. The
revenue arising from his school was small,
and would have been scarcely sufficient to
furnish him with daily bread, for he was a
huge feeder, and, though lank, had the dilat-
ing powers of an anaconda; but to help out his
maintenance he was, according to country
custom in those parts, boarded and lodged at
the houses of the farmers whose children he
instructed. With these he lived successively a
week at a time, thus going the rounds of the
neighborhood with all his worldly effects tied
up in a cotton handkerchief.

That all this might not be too onerous on
the purses of his rustic patrons, who are apt to
consider the costs of schooling a grievous
burden and schoolmasters as mere drones, he
had various ways of rendering himself both

useful and agreeable. He assisted the farmers occasionally in the lighter labors of their farms, helped to make hay, mended the fences, took the horses to water, drove the cows from pasture, and cut wood for the winter fire. He laid aside, too, all the dominant dignity and absolute sway with which he lorded it in his little empire, the school, and became wonderfully gentle and ingratiating. He found favor in the eyes of the mothers by petting the children, particularly the youngest; and like the lion bold, which formerly so magnanimously the lamb did hold, he would sit with a child on one knee and rock a cradle with his foot for whole hours together.

In addition to his other vocations, he was the singing master of the neighborhood and picked up many bright shillings by instructing the young folks in psalmody. It was a matter of no little vanity to him on Sundays to take his station in front of the church gallery with a band of chosen singers, where, in his own

mind, he completely carried away the palm from the parson. Certain it is, his voice resounded far above all the rest of the congregation, and there are peculiar quavers still to be heard in that church, and which may even be heard half a mile off, quite to the opposite side of the mill pond on a still Sunday morning, which are said to be legitimately descended from the nose of Ichabod Crane. Thus, by diverse little makeshifts in that ingenious way which is commonly denominated "by hook and by crook," the worthy pedagogue got on tolerably enough, and was thought, by all who understood nothing of the labor of headwork, to have a wonderfully easy life of it.

The schoolmaster is generally a man of some importance in the female circle of a rural neighborhood, being considered a kind of idle, gentleman-like personage of vastly superior taste and accomplishments to the rough country swains, and, indeed, inferior in learning only to the parson. His appearance, therefore, is apt to occasion some little stir at the tea table of a farmhouse and the addition of a supernumerary dish of cakes or sweetmeats, or, possibly, the parade of a silver teapot. Our man of letters, therefore, was peculiarly happy in the smiles of all the country damsels. How he would figure among them in the churchyard between services on Sundays,

gathering grapes for them from the wild vines that overrun the surrounding trees; reciting for their amusement all the epitaphs on the tombstones; or sauntering, with a whole bevy of them, along the banks of the adjacent mill pond, while the more bashful country bumpkins hung sheepishly back, envying his superior elegance and address.

From his half-itinerant life, also, he was a kind of traveling gazette, carrying the whole budget of local gossip from house to house, so that his appearance was always greeted with satisfaction. He was, moreover, esteemed by the women as a man of great erudition, for he had read several books quite through, and was a perfect master of Cotton Mather's *History of New England Witchcraft,* in which, by the way, he most firmly and potently believed.

He was, in fact, an odd mixture of small shrewdness and simple credulity. His appetite for the marvelous and his powers of digesting it were equally extraordinary, and both had been increased by his residence in this spell-bound region. No tale was too gross or monstrous for his capacious swallow.

It was often his delight, after his school was dismissed in the afternoon, to stretch himself on the rich bed of clover bordering the

little brook that whimpered by his schoolhouse, and there read old Mather's direful
tales until the gathering dusk of the evening
made the printed page a mere mist before his
eyes. Then, as he wended his way by swamp
and stream and awful woodland to the farmhouse where he happened to be quartered,
every sound of Nature at that witching hour
fluttered his excited imagination—the moan
of the whip-poor-will from the hillside; the
boding cry of the tree toad, that harbinger of
storm; the dreary hooting of the screech owl;
or the sudden rustling in the thicket of birds
frightened from their roost. The fireflies, too,
which sparkled most vividly in the darkest
places, now and then startled him as one of
uncommon brightness would stream across
his path; and if, by chance, a huge blockhead
of a beetle came winging his blundering flight
against him, the poor varlet was ready to give
up the ghost, with the idea that he was struck
with a witch's token. His only resource

on such occasions, either to drown thought or drive away evil spirits, was to sing psalm tunes. And the good people of Sleepy Hollow, as they sat by their doors of an evening, were often filled with awe at hearing his nasal melody, "in linked sweetness long drawn out," floating from the distant hill or along the dusky road.

Another of his sources of fearful pleasure

was to pass long winter evenings with the old Dutch wives as they sat spinning by the fire, with a row of apples roasting and spluttering along the hearth, and listen to their marvelous tales of ghosts and goblins, and haunted fields, and haunted brooks, and haunted bridges, and haunted houses, and particularly of the headless horseman, or Galloping Hessian of the Hollow, as they sometimes called him. He would delight them equally by his anecdotes of witchcraft and of the direful omens and portentous sights and sounds in the air which prevailed in the earlier times of Connecticut, and would frighten them woefully with speculations upon comets and shooting stars, and with the alarming fact that the world did absolutely turn around and that they were half the time topsy-turvy.

But if there was a pleasure in all this while snugly cuddling in the chimney corner of a chamber that was all of a ruddy glow from the

crackling wood fire, and where, of course, no specter dared to show its face, it was dearly purchased by the terrors of his subsequent walk homewards. What fearful shapes and shadows beset his path amidst the dim and ghastly glare of a snowy night! With what wistful look did he eye every trembling ray of light steaming across the waste fields from some distant window! How often was he appalled by

some shrub covered with snow, which, like a sheeted specter, beset his very path! How often did he shrink with curdling awe at the sound of his own steps on the frosty

crust beneath his feet, and dread to look over his shoulder, lest he should behold some un-couth being tramping close behind him! And how often was he thrown into complete dismay by some rushing blast howling among the trees, in the idea that it was the Galloping Hessian on one of his nightly scourings!

All these, however, were mere terrors of the night, phantoms of the mind that walk in darkness; and though he had seen many specters in his time, and been more than once beset by Satan in diverse shapes in his lonely perambulations, yet daylight put an end to all these evils; and he would have passed a pleasant life of it, in spite of the

Devil and all his works, if his path had not been crossed by a being that causes more perplexity to mortal man than ghosts, goblins, and the whole race of witches put together, and that was—a woman.

Among the musical disciples who assembled one evening in each week to receive his instructions in psalmody was Katrina Van Tassel, the daughter and only child of a substantial Dutch farmer. She was a blooming lass of fresh eighteen, plump as a partridge, ripe and melting and rosy-cheeked as one of her father's peaches, and universally famed, not merely for her beauty, but for her vast expectations. She was withal a little of a coquette, as might be perceived even in her dress, which was a mixture of ancient and modern fashions, as most suited to set off her charms. She wore the ornaments of pure yellow gold which her great-great-grandmother had brought over from Saardam, the tempting stomacher of the olden time, and a provokingly short petticoat to display the prettiest foot and ankle in the country round.

Ichabod Crane had a soft and foolish heart towards the sex, and it is not to be wondered at that so tempting a morsel soon found favor in his eyes, more especially after he had visited her in her paternal mansion. Old Baltus Van Tassel was a perfect picture of a thriving, contented, liberal-hearted farmer. He seldom, it is true, sent either his eyes or his thoughts beyond the boundaries of his own farm, but within those everything was snug, happy, and well-conditioned. He was satisfied with his wealth, but not proud of it, and prided himself upon the hearty abundance, rather than the style in which he lived.

His stronghold was situated on the banks of the Hudson, in one of those green, sheltered, fertile nooks in which the Dutch farmers are so fond of nestling. A great elm tree spread its broad branches over it, at the foot of which bubbled up a spring of the softest and sweetest water in a little well formed of a barrel, and

then stole sparkling away through the grass to
a neighboring brook that bubbled along
among alders and dwarf willows. Close by
the farmhouse was a vast barn, which might
have served for a church, every window and
crevice of which seemed bursting forth with
the treasures of the farm; the flail was busily
resounding within it from morning to night;
swallows and martins skimmed twittering
about the eaves; and rows of pigeons, some
with one eye turned up, as if watching the
weather, some with their heads under their
wings or buried in their bosoms, and others,
swelling, and cooing, and bowing about their
dames, were enjoying the sunshine on the
roof. Sleek, unwieldly porkers were grunting
in the repose and abundance of their pens,

from where sallied forth, now and then, troops of sucking pigs as if to snuff the air. A stately squadron of snowy geese were riding in an adjoining pond, convoying whole fleets of ducks; regiments of turkeys were gobbling through the farmyard, and guinea fowls fretting about it, like ill-tempered housewives, with their peevish, discontented cry. Before the barn door strutted the gallant cock, that pattern of a husband, a warrior, and a fine gentleman, clapping his burnished wings and crowing in the pride and gladness of his heart—sometimes tearing up the earth with his feet, and then generously calling his ever-hungry family of wives and children to enjoy the rich morsel which he had discovered.

The pedagogue's mouth watered as he looked upon this sumptuous promise of luxurious winter fare. In his devouring mind's eye he pictured to himself every roasting pig running about with a pudding in his belly and an apple in his mouth. The pigeons were snugly put to bed in a comfortable pie and tucked in with a coverlet of crust. The geese were swimming in their own gravy and the ducks pairing cozily in dishes, like snug married couples, with a decent competency of onion sauce. In the porkers he saw carved out the future sleek side of bacon and juicy relishing ham. Not a turkey but he beheld daintily trussed up, with its gizzard under its wing, and, posssibly, a necklace of savory sausages; and even bright Chanticleer himself lay sprawling on his back in a side dish, with uplifted claws, as if craving that quarter which his chivalrous spirit disdained to ask while living.

As the enraptured Ichabod fancied all this, and as he rolled his great green eyes over the fat meadow lands, the rich fields of wheat, of rye, of buckwheat, and Indian corn, and the orchards burdened with ruddy fruit, which surrounded the warm tenement of Van Tassel, his heart yearned after the damsel who was to inherit these domains, and his imagination expanded with the idea how they might be readily turned into cash and the money invested in immense tracts of wild land and shingle palaces in the wilderness. Nay, his busy fancy already realized his hopes, and presented to him the blooming Katrina, with a whole family of children, mounted on the top of a wagon loaded with household trumpery, with pots and kettles dangling beneath, and he beheld himself bestriding a pacing mare, with a colt at her heels, setting out for Kentucky, Tennessee, or the Lord knows where.

When he entered the house the conquest of his heart was complete. It was one of those spacious farmhouses with high-ridged but lowly sloping roofs, built in the style handed down from the first Dutch settlers, the low projecting eaves forming a piazza along the front, capable of being closed up in bad weather. Under this were hung flails, harness, various utensils of husbandry, and nets for fishing in the neighboring river. Benches were built along the sides for summer use, and a great spinning-wheel at one end and a churn at the other showed the various uses to which this important porch might be devoted.

From this piazza the wondering Ichabod entered the hall, which formed the center of the mansion and the place of usual residence. Here rows of resplendent pewter, ranged on a long dresser, dazzled his eyes. In one corner stood a huge bag of wool ready to be spun; in another a quantity of linsey-woolsey just from the loom. Ears of Indian corn and strings of dried apples and peaches hung in gay festoons along the walls, mingled with the gaud of red peppers. And a door left ajar gave him a peep into the best parlor, where the claw-footed chairs and dark mahogany tables shone like mirrors. Andirons, with their accompanying shovel and tongs, glistened from their covert of asparagus tops. Mock oranges and conch shells decorated the mantelpiece. Strings of various colored birds' eggs were suspended above it. A great ostrich egg was hung from the center of the room, and a corner cupboard, knowingly left open, displayed immense treasures of old silver and well-mended china.

From the moment Ichabod laid his eyes upon these regions of delight the peace of his mind was at an end, and his only study was how to gain the affections of the peerless daughter of Van Tassel. In this enterprise, however, he had more real difficulties than generally fell to the lot of a knight-errant of yore, who seldom had anything but giants, enchanters, fiery dragons, and such-like easily conquered adversaries to contend with, and had to make his way merely through gates of iron and brass and impenetrable walls to the castle keep, where the lady of his heart was confined; all which he achieved as easily as a man would carve his way to the center of a Christmas pie, and then the lady gave him her hand as a matter of course. Ichabod, on the contrary, had to win his way to the heart of a country coquette beset with a labyrinth of whims and caprices, which were forever presenting new difficulties and impediments. And he had to encounter a host of fearful adversaries of real flesh and blood, the numerous rustic admirers who beset every portal to her heart, keeping a watchful and angry eye upon each other, but ready to fly out in the common cause against any new competitor.

Among these the most formidable was a burly, roaring, roistering blade of the name of Abraham—or, according to the Dutch abbreviation, Brom—Van Brunt, the hero of the country round, which rang with his feats of strength and hardihood. He was broad-shouldered and double-jointed, with short, curly black hair and a bluff but not unpleasant countenance, having a mingled air of fun and arrogance. From his Herculean frame and great powers of limb, he had received the nickname of Brom Bones, by which he was universally known. He was famed for great knowledge and skill in horsemanship, being as dextrous on horseback as a Tartar. He was foremost at all races and cock fights, and, with the ascendency which bodily strength acquires in rustic life, with the umpire in all disputes, setting his hat on one side and giving his decisions with an air and tone admitting of no gainsay or appeal. He was always ready for either a fight or a frolic, but had more mischief than ill-will in his composition; and with all his overbearing roughness there was a strong dash of waggish good-humor at bottom.

He had three or four boon companions who regarded him as their model, and at the head of whom he scoured the country, attending every scene of feud or merriment for miles around. In cold weather he was distinguished by a fur cap surmounted with a flaunting fox's tail; and when the folks at a country gathering descried this well-known crest at a distance, whisking about among a squad of hard riders, they always stood by for a squall. Sometimes his crew would be heard dashing along past the farmhouses at midnight with hoop and halloo, like a troop of Don Cossacks, and the old dames, startled out of their sleep, would listen for a moment till the hurry-scurry had clattered by, and then exclaim, "Ay, there goes Brom Bones with his gang!" The neighbors looked upon him with a mixture of awe, admiration, and good will, and when any madcap prank or rustic brawl occurred in the vicinity always shook their heads and warranted Brom Bones was at the bottom of it.

This rantipole hero had for some time singled out the blooming Katrina for the object of his uncouth gallantries, and, though his amorous toyings were something like the gentle caresses and endearments of a bear, yet it was whispered that she did not altogether discourage his hopes. Certain it is, his advances were signals for rival candidates to retire who felt no inclination to cross a lion in his amours; insomuch, that when his horse

was seen tied to Van Tassel's paling on a Sunday night, a sure sign that his master was courting—or, as it is termed, "sparking"—within, all other suitors passed by in despair and carried the war into other quarters.

Such was the formidable rival with whom Ichabod Crane had to contend, and, considering all things, a stouter man than he would have shrunk from the competition and a wiser man would have despaired. He had, however, a happy mixture of pliability and perseverance in his nature; he was in form and spirit like a supple jack—yielding, but tough; though he bent, he never broke; and though he bowed beneath the slightest pressure, yet the moment it was away, jerk! he was as erect and carried his head as high as ever.

To have taken the field openly against his rival would have been madness; for he was not a man to be thwarted in his amours, any more than that stormy lover, Achilles. Ichabod, therefore, made his advances in a quiet and gently insinuating manner. Under cover of his character of singing master he made frequent visits at the farmhouse; not that he had anything to apprehend from the meddlesome interference of parents, which is so often a stumbling block in the path of lovers. Balt Van Tassel was an easy, indulgent soul. He loved his daughter better even than his pipe, and, like a reasonable man and an excellent father, let her have her way in everything. His notable little wife, too, had enough to do to attend to her housekeeping and manage her poultry; for, as she sagely observed, ducks and geese are foolish things and must be looked after, but girls can take care of themselves.

Thus while the busy dame bustled about the house or plied her spinning-wheel at one end of the piazza, honest Balt would sit smoking his evening pipe at the other, watching the achievements of a little wooden warrior who, armed with a sword in each hand, was most valiantly fighting the wind on the pinnacle of the barn. In the meantime, Ichabod would carry on his suit with the daughter by the side of the spring under the great elm or sauntering along in the twilight, that hour so favorable to the lover's eloquence.

I profess not to know how women's hearts are wooed and won. To me they have always been matters of riddle and admiration. Some seem to have but one vulnerable point or door of access, while others have a thousand avenues and may be captured in a thousand different ways. It is a great triumph of skill to gain the former, but a still greater proof of generalship to maintain possession of the latter, for a man must battle for his fortress at every door and window. He who wins a thousand common hearts is therefore entitled to some renown, but he who keeps undisputed sway over the heart of a coquette is indeed a hero. Certain it is, this was not the case with the redoubtable Brom Bones; and from the moment Ichabod Crane made his advances the interests of the former evidently declined. His horse was no longer seen tied at the palings on Sunday nights, and a deadly feud gradually arose between him and the preceptor of Sleepy Hollow.

Brom, who had a degree of rough chivalry in his nature, would fain have carried matters to open warfare, and have settled their pretensions to the lady according to the mode of those most concise and simple reasoners, the knights-errant of yore—by single combat. But Ichabod was too conscious of the superior might of his adversary to enter the lists against him: he had overheard a boast of Bones, that he would "double the school-

master up and lay him on a shelf of his own
schoolhouse"; and he was too wary to give
him an opportunity. There was something
extremely provoking in this obstinately pa-
cific system; it left Brom no alternative but
to draw upon the funds of rustic waggery
in his disposition and to play off boorish
practical jokes upon his rival. Ichabod be-

came the object of whimsical persecution to Bones and his gang of rough riders. They harried his hitherto peaceful domains; smoked out his singing school by stopping up the chimney; broke into the schoolhouse at night, in spite of its formidable fastenings of branches and window stakes, and turned everything topsy-turvy; so that the poor schoolmaster began to think all the witches in the country held their meetings there. But, what was still more annoying, Brom took all opportunities of turning him into ridicule in the presence of Katrina, and had a scoundrel dog whom he taught to whine in the most ludicrous manner, and introduced as a rival of Ichabod's to instruct her in psalmody.

In this way matters went on for some time without producing any material effect on the relative situation of the contending powers. On a fine autumnal afternoon Ichabod, in a pensive mood, sat enthroned on the lofty stool from which he usually watched all the concerns of his little literary realm. In his

hand he swayed a ferule, that scepter of
despotic power. The birch of justice reposed
on three nails behind the throne, a constant
terror to evildoers, while on the desk before
him might be seen sundry contraband articles

and prohibited weapons detected upon the persons of idle urchins, such as half-munched apples, popguns, whirligigs, fly cages, and whole legions of rampant little paper game-cocks.

Apparently there had been some appalling act of justice recently inflicted, for his scholars were all busily intent upon their books or slyly whispering behind them with one eye kept upon the master, and a kind of buzzing stillness reigned throughout the schoolroom. It was suddenly interrupted by the appearance of a Negro in tow-cloth jacket and trousers, a round-crowned fragment of a hat like the cap of Mercury, and mounted on the back of a ragged, wild, half-broken colt, which he managed with a rope by way of halter. He came clattering up to the school door with an invitation to Ichabod to attend a merrymaking or "quilting frolic" to be held that evening at Mynheer Van Tassel's. Having delivered his message with an air of importance, he dashed over the brook, and was seen scampering away up the hollow, full of importance and hurry of his mission.

All was now bustle and hubbub in the schoolroom. The scholars were hurried through their lessons without stopping at trifles. Those who were nimble skipped over half with impunity, and those who were tardy had a smart application now and then in the rear to quicken their speed or help them over a tall word. Books were flung aside without being put away on the shelves, inkstands were overturned, benches thrown down, and the whole school was turned loose an hour before the usual time, bursting forth like a legion of young imps, yelping and racketing about the green in joy at their early emancipation.

The gallant Ichabod now spent at least an extra half hour at his toilet, brushing and furbishing up his best, and indeed only, suit of rusty black, and arranging his looks by a bit of broken looking glass that hung in the school-house. That he might make his appearance before his mistress in the true style of a cavalier, he borrowed a horse from the farmer with whom he was staying, a choleric old Dutchman of the name of Hans Van Ripper, and, thus gallantly mounted, issued forth like a knight errant in quest of adventures.

But it is proper that I should, in the true spirit of romantic story, give some account of the looks and equipment of my hero and his steed. The animal he bestrode was a broken-down plough horse that had outlived almost everything but his viciousness. He was gaunt and shaggy, with a ewe neck and a head like a hammer. His rusty mane and tail were tangled and knotted with burrs. One eye had lost its pupil and was glaring and spectral, but the other had the gleam of a genuine devil in it. Still, he must have had fire and mettle in his day, if we may judge from the name he bore of Gunpowder. He had, in fact, been a favorite steed of his master's, the choleric Van Ripper, who was a furious rider, and had infused, very probably, some of his own spirit into the

animal; for, old and broken down as he looked, there was more of the lurking devil in him than in any young filly in the country.

Ichabod was a suitable figure for such a steed. He rode with short stirrups, which brought his knees nearly up to the pommel of the saddle. His sharp elbows stuck out like grasshoppers'. He carried his whip perpendicularly in his hand like a scepter. And as his horse jogged on, the motion of his arms was not unlike the flapping of a pair of wings. A small wool hat rested on the top of his nose, for so his scanty strip of forehead might be called, and the skirts of his black coat fluttered out almost to his horse's tail. Such was the appearance of Ichabod and his steed as they shambled out of the gate of Hans Van Ripper, and it was altogether such an apparition as is seldom to be met with in broad daylight.

It was, as I have said, a fine autumnal day, the sky was clear and serene, and Nature wore that rich and golden livery which we always associate with the idea of abundance. The forests had put on their sober brown and yellow, while some trees of the tenderer kind had been nipped by the frosts into brilliant dyes of orange, purple, and scarlet. Streaming files of wild ducks began to make their appearance high in the air. The bark of the squirrel might be heard from the groves of beech and hickory nuts, and the pensive whistle of the quail at intervals from the neighboring stubble field.

The small birds were taking their farewell banquets. In the fullness of their revelry they fluttered, chirping and frolicking, from bush to bush and tree to tree, capricious from the very profusion and variety around them. There was the honest cock robin, the favorite game of stripling sportsmen, with its loud querulous note; and the twittering blackbirds, flying in sable clouds; and the golden-winged

woodpecker, with his crimson crest, his broad black gorget, and splendid plumage; and the cedar bird, with its red-tipped wings and yellow-tipped tail and its little monteiro cap of feathers; and the blue jay, that noisy coxcomb, in his gay light-blue coat and white underclothes, screaming and chattering, nodding and bobbing and bowing, and pretending to be on good terms with every songster of the grove.

As Ichabod jogged slowly on his way, his eyes, ever open to every symptom of culinary abundance, ranged with delight over the treasures of jolly autumn. On all sides he beheld vast store of apples—some hanging in oppressive opulence on the trees, some gathered into baskets and barrels for the market, others heaped up in rich piles for the cider press. Farther on he beheld great fields of Indian corn, with its golden ears peeping from their leafy coverts and holding out the promise of cakes and hasty pudding; and the yellow pumpkins lying beneath them, turning up their fair round bellies to the sun, and giving ample prospects of the most luxurious of pies. And soon he passed the fragrant buckwheat fields, breathing the odor of the beehive, and as he beheld them soft anticipations stole over his mind of dainty slapjacks, well-buttered and garnished with honey or treacle by the delicate little dimpled hand of Katrina Van Tassel.

Thus feeding his mind with many sweet thoughts and "sugared suppositions," he journeyed along the sides of a range of hills which look out upon some of the goodliest scenes of the mighty Hudson.

The sun gradually wheeled his broad disk down into the west. The wide bosom of the Tappan Zee lay motionless and glassy, except that here and there a gentle undulation waved and prolonged the blue shadow of the distant mountain. A few amber clouds floated in the sky, without a breath of air to move them. The horizon was of a fine golden tint, changing gradually into a pure apple green, and from that into the deep blue of the mid-heaven. A slanting ray lingered on the woody crests of the precipices that overhung some parts of the river, giving greater depth to the dark gray and purple of their rocky sides. A sloop was loitering in the distance, dropping slowly down with the tide, her sail hanging uselessly against the mast, and as the reflection of the sky gleamed along the still water it seemed as if the vessel was suspended in the air.

It was toward evening that Ichabod arrived at the castle of the Heer Van Tassel, which he found thronged with the pride and flower of the adjacent country—old farmers, a spare leather-faced race, in homespun coats and breeches, blue stockings, huge shoes, and magnificent pewter buckles; their brisk withered little dames, in close crimped caps, long-waisted shortgowns, homespun petticoats, with scissors and pincushions and gay calico pockets hanging on the outside; buxom lasses, almost as antiquated as their mothers, except where a straw hat, a fine ribbon, or perhaps a white frock gave symptoms of city innovation; the sons, in short square-skirted coats with rows of stupendous brass buttons, and their hair generally braided in the fashion of the times, especially if they could procure an eel skin for the purpose, it being esteemed throughout the country as a potent nourisher and strengthener of the hair.

Brom Bones, however, was the hero of the scene, having come to the gathering on his favorite steed Daredevil—a creature, like himself, full of metal and mischief, and which no one but himself could manage. He was, in fact, noted for preferring vicious animals, given to all kinds of tricks, which kept the rider in constant risk of his neck, for he held a tractable, well-broken horse as unworthy of a lad of spirit.

Fain would I pause to dwell upon the world of charms that burst upon the enraptured gaze of my hero as he entered the state parlor of Van Tassel's mansion. Not those of the bevy of buxom lasses with their luxurious display of red and white, but the ample charms of a genuine Dutch country tea table in the sumptuous time of autumn. Such heaped-up platters of cakes of various and almost indescribable kinds, known only to experienced Dutch housewives! There was the doughty doughnut, the tenderer oly koek, and the crisp and crumbling cruller; sweet cakes and short cakes, ginger cakes and honey cakes, and the whole family of cakes. And then there were apple pies and peach pies and pumpkin pies, besides slices of ham and smoked beef; and moreover delectable dishes of preserved plums and peaches and pears and quinces, not to mention broiled shad and roasted chickens, together with bowls of milk and cream—all mingled higgledy-piggledy, pretty much as I have enumerated them, with the motherly teapot sending up its clouds of vapor from the midst. Heaven bless the mark! I want breath and time to discuss this banquet as it deserves, and am too eager to get on with my story. Happily, Ichabod Crane was not in so great a hurry as his historian, but did ample justice to every dainty.

He was a kind and thankful creature, whose heart dilated in proportion as his skin was filled with good cheer, and whose spirits rose with eating as some men's do with drink. He could not help, too, rolling his large eyes round him as he ate, and chuckling with the possibility that he might one day be lord of all this scene of almost unimaginable luxury and splendor. Then, he thought, how soon he'd turn his back upon the old schoolhouse, snap his fingers in the face of Hans Van Ripper and every other miserly patron, and kick any itinerant pedagogue out of doors that should dare to call him comrade!

Old Baltus Van Tassel moved about among his guests with a face dilated with content and good humor, round and jolly as the harvest moon. His hospitable attentions were brief, but expressive, being confined to a shake of the hand, a slap on the shoulder, a loud laugh, and a pressing invitation to "fall to and help themselves."

And now the sound of music from the common room, or hall, summoned to the dance. The musician was an old gray-headed Negro who had been the itinerant orchestra of the neighborhood for more than half a century. His instrument was as old and battered as himself. The greater part of the time he scraped on two or three strings, accompanying every movement of the bow with a motion of the head, bowing almost to the ground and stamping with his foot whenever a fresh couple were to start.

Ichabod prided himself upon his dancing as much as upon his vocal powers. Not a limb, not a fiber about him was idle; and to have seen his loosely hung frame in full motion and clattering about the room you would have thought Saint Vitus himself, that blessed patron of the dance, was figuring before you in person. He was the admiration of all the Negroes, who, having gathered, of all ages and sizes, from the farm and the neighborhood, stood forming a pyramid of shining black faces at every door and window, gazing with delight at the scene and grinning from ear to ear.

How could the flogger of urchins be otherwise than animated and joyous! The lady of his heart was his partner in the dance, and smiling graciously in reply to all his amorous oglings, while Brom Bones, sorely smitten with love and jealousy, sat brooding by himself in one corner.

When the dance was at an end Ichabod was attracted to a knot of the sager folks, who, with old Van Tassel, sat smoking at one end of the piazza gossiping over former times and drawing out long stories about the war.

This neighborhood, at the time of which I am speaking, was one of those highly favored places which abound with chronicle and great men. The British and American line had run near it during the war. It had therefore been the scene of marauding, and infested with refugees, cowboys, and all kinds of border chivalry. Just sufficient time had elapsed to enable each storyteller to dress up his tale with a little becoming fiction, and in the indistinctness of his recollection to make himself the hero of every exploit.

There was the story of Doffue Martling, a large blue-bearded Dutchman, who had nearly taken a British frigate with an old iron nine-pounder from a mud breastwork, only that his gun burst at the sixth discharge. And there was an old gentleman who shall be nameless, being too rich a mynheer to be lightly mentioned, who, in the battle of Whiteplains, being an excellent master of defense, parried a musket ball with a small sword, insomuch that he absolutely felt it whiz round the blade and glance off at the hilt: in proof of which he was ready at any time to show the sword, with the hilt a little bent. There were several more that had been equally great in the field, not one of whom but was persuaded that he had a considerable hand in bringing the war to a happy termination.

But all these were nothing to the tales of ghosts and apparitions that succeeded. The neighborhood is rich in legendary treasures of the kind. Local tales and superstitions thrive

best in these sheltered, long-settled retreats, but are trampled under foot by the shifting throng that forms the population of most of our country places. Besides, there is no encouragement for ghosts in most of our villages, for they have scarcely had time to finish their first nap and turn themselves in their graves before their surviving friends have traveled away from the neighborhood; so that when they turn out at night to walk their rounds they have no acquaintance left to call upon. This is perhaps the reason why we so seldom hear of ghosts except in our long-established Dutch communities.

The immediate cause, however, of the prevalence of supernatural stories in these parts was doubtless owing to the vicinity of Sleepy Hollow. There was a contagion in the very air that blew from that haunted region. It breathed forth an atmosphere of dreams and fancies infecting all the land. Several of the Sleepy Hollow people were present at Van Tassel's, and, as usual, were doling out their wild and wonderful legends. Many dismal tales were told about funeral trains, and mourning cries and wailings heard and seen about the great tree where the unfortunate Major André was taken, and which stood in the neighborhood. Some mention was made also of the woman in white who haunted the dark glen at Raven Rock, and was often heard

to shriek on winter nights before a storm, having perished there in the snow. The chief part of the stories, however, turned upon the favorite specter of Sleepy Hollow, the head-less horseman, who had been heard several times of late patroling the country, and, it was said, tethered his horse nightly among the graves in the churchyard.

The sequestered situation of this church seems always to have made it a favorite haunt of troubled spirits. It stands on a knoll surrounded by locust trees and lofty elms, from among which its decent whitewashed walls shine modestly forth, like Christian purity beaming through the shades of retirement. A gentle slope descends from it to a silver sheet of water bordered by high trees, between which peeps may be caught at the blue hills of the Hudson. To look upon its grass-grown yard, where the sunbeams seem to sleep so quietly, one would think that there at least the dead might rest in peace.

On one side of the church extends a wide woody dell, along which raves a large brook among broken rocks and trunks of fallen trees. Over a deep black part of the stream, not far from the church, was formerly thrown a wooden bridge. The road that led to it

and the bridge itself were thickly shaded by overhanging trees, which cast a gloom about it even in the daytime, but occasioned a fearful darkness at night. Such was one of the favorite haunts of the headless horseman, and the place where he was most frequently encountered. The tale was told of old Brouwer, a most heretical disbeliever in ghosts, how he met the horseman returning from his foray into Sleepy

Hollow, and was obliged to get up behind him; how they galloped over bush and brake, over hill and swamp, until they reached the bridge, when the horseman suddenly turned into a skeleton, threw old Brouwer into the brook, and sprang away over the treetops with a clap of thunder.

This story was immediately matched by a thrice-marvelous adventure of Brom Bones, who made light of the galloping Hessian as an arrant jockey. He affirmed that on returning one night from the neighboring village of Sing-Sing he had been overtaken by this midnight trooper; that he had offered to race with him for a bowl of punch, and should have won it too, for Daredevil beat the goblin horse all hollow, but just as they came to the church bridge the Hessian bolted and vanished in a flash of fire.

All these tales, told in that drowsy undertone with which men talk in the dark, the countenances of the listeners only now and then receiving a casual gleam from the glare of a pipe, sank deep in the mind of Ichabod. He repaid them in kind with large extracts from his invaluable author, Cotton Mather, and added many marvelous events that had taken place in his native state of Connecticut, and fearful sights which he had seen in his nightly walks about Sleepy Hollow.

The revel now gradually broke up. The old farmers gathered together their families in their wagons, and were heard for some time rattling along the hollow roads and over the distant hills. Some of the damsels mounted on pillions behind their favorite swains, and their lighthearted laughter, mingling with the clatter of hoofs, echoed along the silent woodlands, sounding fainter and fainter until they gradually died away, and the late scene of noise and frolic was all silent and deserted.

Only Ichabod lingered behind, according to the custom of country lovers, to have a tête-à-tête with the heiress, fully convinced that he was now on the high road to success.

What passed at this interview I will not pretend to say, for in fact I do not know. Something, however, I fear, must have gone wrong, for he certainly sallied forth, after no very great interval, with an air quite desolate and crestfallen. Oh these women! These women! Could that girl have been playing off any of her coquettish tricks? Was her encouragement of the poor pedagogue all a mere sham to secure her conquest of his rival? Heaven only knows, not I! Let it suffice to say, Ichabod stole forth with the air of one who had been sacking a hen-roost rather than a fair lady's heart. Without looking to the right or left to notice the scene of rural wealth on which he had so often gloated, he went straight to the stable, and with several hearty cuffs and kicks roused his steed most uncourteously from the comfortable quarters in which he was soundly sleeping, dreaming of mountains of corn and oats and whole valleys of timothy and clover.

It was the very witching time of night that

Ichabod, heavy-hearted and crestfallen, pursued his travel homeward along the sides of the lofty hills which rise above Tarry Town, and which he had traversed so cheerily in the afternoon.

The hour was as dismal as himself. Far below him the Tappan Zee spread its dusky and indistinct waste of waters, with here and there the tall mast of a sloop riding quietly at anchor under the land. In the dead hush of midnight he could even hear the barking of the watchdog from the opposite shore of the Hudson, but it was so vague and faint as only to give an idea of his distance from this faithful companion of man. Now and then, too, the long-drawn crowing of a cock, accidentally awakened, would sound far, far off, from some farmhouse away among the hills, but it was like a dreaming sound in his ear. No signs of life occurred near him, but occasionally the melancholy chirp of a cricket, or perhaps the guttural twang of a bullfrog from a neighboring marsh, as if sleeping uncomfortably and turning suddenly in his bed.

All the stories of ghosts and goblins that he had heard in the afternoon now came crowding upon his recollection. The night grew darker and darker. The stars seemed to sink deeper in the sky, and driving clouds occasionally hid them from his sight. He had never felt so lonely and dismal. He was, moreover, approaching the very place where many of the scenes of the ghost stories had been laid.

In the center of the road stood an enormous tulip tree which towered like a giant above all the other trees of the neighborhood and

formed a kind of landmark. Its limbs were gnarled and fantastic, large enough to form trunks for ordinary trees, twisting down almost to the earth and rising again into the air. It was connected with the tragical story of the unfortunate André, who had been taken prisoner nearby, and was universally known by the name of Major André's tree. The common people regarded it with a mixture of respect and superstition, partly out of sympathy for the fate of its ill-starred namesake, and partly from the tales of strange sights and doleful lamentations told concerning it.

As Ichabod approached this fearful tree he began to whistle: he thought his whistle was answered; it was but a blast sweeping sharply through the dry branches. As he approached a little nearer he thought he saw something white hanging in the midst of the tree. He paused and ceased whistling, but on looking more narrowly perceived that it was a place where the tree had been scathed by light-

ning and the white wood laid bare. Suddenly he heard a groan. His teeth chattered and his knees smote against the saddle; it was but the rubbing of one huge bough upon another as they were swayed about by the breeze. He passed the tree in safety, but new perils lay before him.

About two hundred yards from the tree a small brook crossed the road and ran into a marshy and thickly wooded glen known by the name of Wiley's Swamp. A few rough logs, laid side by side, served as a bridge over this stream. On that side of the road where the brook entered the wood a group of oaks and chestnuts, matted thick with wild grapevines, threw a cavernous gloom over it. To pass this bridge was the severest trial. It was at this identical spot that the unfortunate André was captured, and under the covert of those chestnuts and vines were the sturdy yeomen concealed who surprised him. This has ever since been considered a haunted stream, and fearful are the feelings of a schoolboy who has to pass it alone after dark.

As he approached the stream his heart began to thump. He summoned up, however, all his resolution, gave his horse half a score of kicks in the ribs, and attempted to dash briskly across the bridge. But instead of starting forward, the perverse old animal made a lateral movement and ran broadside against the fence. Ichabod, whose fears increased with the delay, jerked the reins on the other side and kicked lustily with the contrary foot. It was all in vain; his steed started, it is true, but it was only to plunge to the opposite side of the road into a thicket of brambles and alderbushes. The schoolmaster now bestowed both whip and heel upon the starveling ribs of old Gunpowder, who dashed forward, snuffing and snorting, but came to a stand just by the bridge with a suddenness that had nearly sent his rider sprawling over his head.

Just at this moment a plashy tramp by the

side of the bridge caught the sensitive ear of Ichabod. In the dark shadow of the grove on the margin of the brook he beheld something huge, misshapen, black, and towering. It stirred not, but seemed gathered up in the gloom, like some gigantic monster ready to spring upon the traveler.

The hair of the affrighted pedagogue rose upon his head with terror. What was to be done? To turn and fly was now too late. And besides, what chance was there of escaping the ghost or goblin, if such it was, which could ride upon the wings of the wind? Summoning up, therefore, a show of courage, he demanded in stammering accents, "Who are you?" He received no reply. He repeated his demand in a still more agitated voice. Still there was no answer. Once more he cudgeled the sides of the inflexible Gunpowder, and, shutting his eyes, broke forth with involuntary fervor into a psalm tune.

Just then the shadowy object of alarm put

itself in motion, and with a scramble and a bound stood at once in the middle of the road. Though the night was dark and dismal, yet the form of the unknown might now in some degree be ascertained. He appeared to be a horseman of large dimensions and mounted on a black horse of powerful frame. He made no offer of molestation or sociability, but kept aloof on one side of the road, jogging along on the blind side of old Gunpowder, who had now got over his fright and waywardness.

Ichabod, who had no relish for this strange midnight companion, and bethought himself of the adventure of Brom Bones with the galloping Hessian, now quickened his steed in hopes of leaving him behind. The stranger, however, quickened his horse to an equal pace. Ichabod pulled up, and fell into a walk, thinking to lag behind. The other did the same. His heart began to sink within him. He endeavored to resume his psalm tune, but his parched tongue clove to the roof of his mouth and he could not utter a stave. There was something in the moody and dogged silence of this pertinacious companion that was mysterious and appalling. It was soon fearfully accounted for.

On mounting a rising ground, which brought the figure of his fellow traveler in relief against the sky, gigantic in height and muffled in a cloak, Ichabod was horrorstruck on perceiving that he was headless! But his horror was still more increased on observing that the head, which should have rested on his shoulders, was carried before him on the pommel of the saddle. His terror rose to desperation. He rained a shower of kicks and blows upon Gunpowder, hoping by a sudden movement to give his companion the slip; but the specter started full jump with him. Away, then, they dashed through thick and thin, stones flying and sparks flashing at every bound. Ichabod's flimsy garments fluttered in the air as he stretched his long, lanky body away over his horse's head in the eagerness of his flight.

They had now reached the road which turns off to Sleepy Hollow. But Gunpowder, who seemed possessed with a demon, instead of keeping up it, made an opposite turn and plunged headlong downhill to the left. This road leads through a sandy hollow shaded by trees for about a quarter of a mile, where it crosses the bridge famous in goblin story, and just beyond swells the green knoll on which stands the whitewashed church.

As yet the panic of the steed had given his unskillful rider an apparent advantage in the chase. But just as he had got halfway through the hollow the girths of the saddle gave way and he felt it slipping from under him. He seized it by the pommel and endeavored to hold it firm, but in vain, and had just time to save himself by clasping old Gunpowder round the neck, when the saddle fell to the earth, and he heard it trampled under foot by

his pursuer. For a moment the terror of Hans
Van Ripper's wrath passed across his mind,
for it was his Sunday saddle. But this was no
time for petty fears. The goblin was hard on
his haunches, and (unskilled rider that he was)
he had much ado to maintain his seat, sometimes slipping on one side, sometimes on
another, and sometimes jolted on the high
ridge of his horse's backbone with a violence
that he feared would cleave him asunder.

An opening in the trees now cheered him
with the hopes that the church bridge was at
hand. The wavering reflection of a silver star
in the bosom of the brook told him that he
was not mistaken. He saw the walls of the
church dimly glaring under the trees beyond.
He recollected the place where Brom Bones's
ghostly competitor had disappeared.

If I can but reach that bridge, thought
Ichabod, I am safe.

Just then he heard the black steed panting

and blowing close behind him. He even fancied that he felt his hot breath. Another convulsive kick in the ribs, and old Gunpowder sprang upon the bridge. He thundered over the resounding planks; he gained the opposite side; and now Ichabod cast a look behind to see if his pursuer should vanish, according to rule, in a flash of fire and brimstone. Just then he saw the goblin rising in his stirrups and in the very act of hurling his head at him.

Ichabod tried to dodge the horrible missile, but too late. It encountered his cranium with a tremendous crash. He was tumbled headlong into the dust, and Gunpowder, the black steed, and the goblin rider passed by like a whirlwind.

The next morning the old horse was found, without his saddle and with the bridle under his feet, soberly cropping the grass at his master's gate. Ichabod did not make his appearance at breakfast. Dinner hour came, but no Ichabod. The boys assembled at the schoolhouse and strolled idly about the banks of the brook, but no schoolmaster.

Hans Van Ripper now began to feel some uneasiness about the fate of poor Ichabod and his saddle. An inquiry was set on foot, and after diligent investigation the came upon his traces. In one part of the road leading to the church was found the saddle trampled in the dirt. The tracks of horses' hoofs, deeply dented in the road and evidently at furious speed, were traced to the bridge, beyond which, on the bank of a broad part of the brook, where the water ran deep and black, was found the hat of the unfortunate Ichabod, and close beside it a shattered pumpkin.

The brook was searched, but the body of the schoolmaster was not to be discovered. Hans Van Ripper, as executor of his estate, examined the bundle which contained all his worldly effects. They consisted of two shirts and a half, two stocks for the neck, a pair or two of worsted stockings, an old pair of corduroy small-clothes, a rusty razor, a book of psalm tunes full of dog's ears, and a broken pitchpipe. As to the books and furniture of the schoolhouse, they belonged to the community, except Cotton Mather's *History of Witchcraft,* a *New England Almanac,* and a book of dreams and fortunetelling, in which there was a sheet of foolscap much scribbled and blotted in several fruitless attempts to make a copy of verses in honor of the heiress of Van Tassel. These magic books and the poetic scrawl were forthwith consigned to the flames by Hans Van Ripper, who from that time forward determined to send his children no more to school, observing that he never knew any good to come of this same reading and writing. Whatever money the schoolmaster possessed—and he had received his quarter's pay but a day or two before—he must have had about his person at the time of his disappearance.

The mysterious event caused much specu-
lation at the church on the following Sunday.
Knots of gazers and gossips were collected in
the churchyard, at the bridge, and at the spot
where the hat and pumpkin had been found.
The stories of Brouwer, of Bones, and a
whole budget of others were called to mind,
and when they had diligently considered them
all, and compared them with the symptoms of
the present case, they shook their heads and
came to the conclusion that Ichabod had been
carried off by the galloping Hessian. As he
was a bachelor and in nobody's debt, nobody
troubled his head any more about him, the
school was removed to a different quarter of
the hollow, and another pedagogue reigned in
his stead.

It is true an old farmer, who had been
down to New York on a visit several years
after, and from whom this account of the
ghostly adventure was received, brought
home the intelligence that Ichabod Crane

was still alive; that he had left the neighborhood, partly through fear of the goblin and Hans Van Ripper, and partly in mortification at having been suddenly dismissed by the heiress; that he had changed his quarters to a distant part of the country; had kept school and studied law at the same time, had been admitted to the bar, turned politician, electioneered, written for the newspapers, and finally had been made a justice of the Ten Pound Court. Brom Bones, too, who shortly after his rival's disappearance conducted the blooming Katrina in triumph to the altar, was observed to look exceedingly knowing whenever the story of Ichabod was related, and always burst into a hearty laugh at the mention of the pumpkin, which led some to suspect that he knew more about the matter than he chose to tell.

The old country wives, however, who are the best judges of these matters, maintain to this day that Ichabod was spirited away by supernatural means. And it is a favorite story often told about the neighborhood round the winter evening fire. The bridge became more than ever an object of superstitious awe, and that may be the reason why the road has been altered of late years so as to approach the church by the border of the mill pond. The schoolhouse, being deserted, soon fell to decay, and was reported to be haunted by the ghost of the unfortunate pedagogue. And the ploughboy, loitering homeward on a still summer evening, has often fancied his voice at a distance chanting a melancholy psalm tune among the tranquil solitudes of Sleepy Hollow.

Postscript

FOUND IN THE HANDWRITING OF MR. KNICKERBOCKER

The preceding tale is given almost in the precise words in which I heard it related at a Corporation meeting of the ancient city of Manhattoes, at which were present many of its sagest and most illustrious burghers. The narrator was a pleasant, shabby, gentlemanly old fellow in pepper-and-salt clothes, with a sadly humorous face, and one whom I strongly suspected of being poor, he made such efforts to be entertaining.

When his story was concluded there was much laughter and approbation, particularly from two or three deputy aldermen who had been asleep the greater part of the time. There was, however, one tall, dry-looking old gentleman, with beetling eyebrows, who maintained a grave and rather severe face throughout, now and then folding his arms, inclining his head, and looking down upon the floor, as if turning a doubt over in his mind. He was one of your wary men, who never laugh but upon good grounds—when they have reason and the law on their side.

When the mirth of the rest of the company had subsided and silence was restored, he leaned one arm on the elbow of his chair, and, sticking the other akimbo, demanded, with a slight but exceedingly sage motion of the head and contraction of the brow, what was the moral of the story and what it went to prove.

The storyteller, who was just putting a glass of wine to his lips as a refreshment after his toils, paused for a moment, looked at his inquirer with an air of infinite deference, and, lowering the glass slowly to the table, observed that the story was intended most logically to prove—

"That there is no situation in life but has its advantages and pleasures—provided we will but take a joke as we find it.

"That, therefore, he that runs races with goblin troopers is likely to have rough riding of it.

"Ergo, for a country schoolmaster to be refused the hand of a Dutch heiress is a certain step to high preferment in the state."

The cautious old gentleman knit his brows tenfold closer after this explanation, being sorely puzzled by the ratiocination of the syllogism, while methought the one in pepper-

and–salt eyed him with something of a trium-
phant leer. At length he observed that all this
was very well, but still he thought the story a
little extravagant—there were one or two
points on which he had his doubts.

"Faith, sir," replied the storyteller, "as to
that matter, I don't believe one half of it
myself." D. K.

Enjoy all of these American Girl Mysteries®:

THE SILENT STRANGER   A *Kaya* Mystery

LADY MARGARET'S GHOST   A *Felicity* Mystery

SECRETS IN THE HILLS   A *Josefina* Mystery

THE RUNAWAY FRIEND   A *Kirsten* Mystery

SHADOWS ON SOCIETY HILL   An *Addy* Mystery

THE CRY OF THE LOON   A *Samantha* Mystery

A THIEF IN THE THEATER   A *Kit* Mystery

CLUES IN THE SHADOWS   A *Molly* Mystery

THE TANGLED WEB   A *Julie* Mystery

and many more!

— A *Felicity* MYSTERY —

LADY MARGARET'S GHOST

by Elizabeth McDavid Jones

★ American Girl®

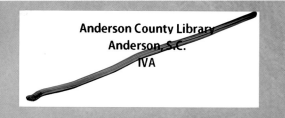

Questions or comments? Call 1-800-845-0005, visit our
Web site at **americangirl.com**, or write to Customer Service,
American Girl, 8400 Fairway Place, Middleton, WI 53562-0497.

Printed in China
09 10 11 12 13 14 LEO 10 9 8 7 6 5 4 3 2 1

PICTURE CREDITS

The following individuals and organizations have generously
given permission to reprint illustrations contained in "Looking Back":
pp. 164–165—street scene, detail from a photograph copyright © 1999 by
Russ Kendall from *Mary Geddy's Day: A Colonial Girl in Williamsburg* by
Kate Waters. Reprinted by permission of Scholastic Inc.; girl with basket,
Colonial Williamsburg Foundation; pp. 166–167—Publick Times scene and
racing horses, Colonial Williamsburg Foundation; pp. 168–169—escaping
thief, Colonial Williamsburg Foundation; pp. 170–171—girl with basket,
Colonial Williamsburg Foundation; almshouse, Bettmann/Corbis;
weaver, © Jan Butchofsky-Houser/Corbis.

Illustrations by Jean-Paul Tibbles

Cataloging-in-Publication Data
available from the Library of Congress.

To Lynne Garcia,
who helped my lost boy find the light

Table of Contents

1
A DELIVERY

"Mother, please don't worry about us while you're gone." Felicity Merriman was trying her best to sound more confident than she felt. She was standing with her father and his apprentice, Ben, outside their white clapboard house in Williamsburg.

The coach that was waiting to take Mother and the younger children away for two weeks was loaded with their trunks and bags. The driver was on top, and the horses were stamping their feet, eager to be off. Nan, William, and baby Polly were aboard, and so was Rose, the family servant, who was going along to help care for Polly. They were all going to visit Mother's elderly Aunt Prudence.

Even so early on this October morning,

Lady Margaret's Ghost

Duke of Gloucester Street, where Felicity's family lived, was bustling. This was the middle week of Publick Times, when the high court was in session and people from all over Virginia flocked to town. Each day, important-looking men walked past Felicity's house to the redbrick capitol building to attend court. Fine ladies and gentlemen in brightly colored clothes strolled the sidewalks and stopped in the shops and businesses. Carts, carriages, and horses with riders filled the street.

Mother gave Felicity one last hug. "I'm not worried. If you'll but pay attention to the task at hand, instead of slipping off into daydreams, you'll be fine. I'm sure you'll live up to my expectations. After all, you're nearly grown, and quite capable of managing a household on your own for two weeks."

Felicity took a breath to calm the fluttery butterflies in her stomach. Mother *had* been giving her more responsibility since Felicity's eleventh birthday this past spring. Although she was still allowed to spend time with her horses, Penny and Patriot, and her best friend, Elizabeth Cole, Felicity now spent more of each day working alongside Mother, learning to run the household.

But could she do it all alone—without Mother and Rose to consult—for two weeks? She didn't want Mother to know how nervous she was at the prospect.

As if reading her thoughts, Mother went on, "And you'll have Mrs. Hewitt to help you with the cooking. She should be arriving later this morning."

Oh, yes. Felicity had nearly forgotten about the elderly widow Mother had hired to come a few hours a day to help Felicity prepare meals.

"I hope Mrs. Hewitt is a good cook," Ben commented. Ben lived with the Merrimans and worked in the store Father owned. Ben looked forward to meals almost as much as he looked forward to his eighteenth birthday, when Father would allow him to join the Patriot army. It was 1776, and the colonies had been at war with England for more than a year.

"You have nothing to fear, Ben," Father said with a smile. "Mrs. Hewitt comes highly recommended. In her younger years, she cooked for the governor at the palace." Father offered his hand to Mother. "My dear, we mustn't delay you. 'Tis two days' journey to Norfolk, and Aunt Prudence expects you before dark tomorrow."

As Father helped Mother board the coach, Nan stuck her head and shoulders out the window and said to Felicity, "How I wish I could stay home with you, Lissie, and watch Ben ride Penny in the race tomorrow! You'll give Penny an extra lump of sugar beforehand, won't you, and say it's from me?"

"Of course," Felicity promised. Her heart beat faster thinking of the race. The horse races were one of the most exciting events of Publick Times. People came from miles around Williamsburg to enter their animals or to watch the competition. Felicity hoped that Penny would win the prize for first place.

Felicity squeezed Nan's hand. "You'll help Mother with the little ones, won't you, lamb?

A Delivery

Father's eyes twinkled. "Lissie, my dear, you can always sense a story. There is indeed one behind Lady Margaret. But first let me show you her belongings. They're part of the tale."

Father placed the trunk on the table beside Felicity and lifted the lid. "Oh," Felicity breathed. On a bed of purple velvet lay a woman's silver vanity set, inlaid with tiny emeralds: a hairbrush, a comb, and several delicate hair ornaments. Beside the vanity set was a child's cup of glistening silver and an infant's silver rattle.

Ben gave a soft, low whistle. "Holy month of Sundays. Looks as if that silver could finance the whole Patriot army. It must be worth a fortune."

"Lady Margaret's belongings *are* very valuable," Father said. "And I'm afraid I shall have to sell them, if I can find a buyer. The war has brought hard times to everyone, and storekeepers are no exception. Whatever money I can get for the heirlooms will be very useful."

Felicity could only stare at the heirlooms. She'd never seen such fine, beautiful silver pieces.

Gingerly she touched the lustrous silver back
of the brush and ran her fingers over the tiny,
sparkling emeralds. In the sunshine through the
window, the jewels glinted and winked like cat's
eyes. An unexplained chill snaked down Felicity's
spine, and her fingers seemed to tingle. Startled,
she jerked her hand away from the brush.

"Are you all right, Lissie?" Ben asked.

"I . . . um . . . had a cramp," she stammered,
massaging her fingers with the other hand. She
felt foolish. Surely the tingling had been her
imagination. Quickly she changed the subject.
"Father, tell us about Lady Margaret. You've said
the brush and comb and hair ornaments were
hers. The cup and rattle must have belonged to
her baby."

"That's the tragedy of it," Father said. "Lady
Margaret desperately wanted to give her beloved
husband a child. Edward was the last Merriman,
you see. If he died without a son, the family
name would die with him.

"Margaret finally had a baby—a boy—but
he was stillborn. The birth was difficult, and

Margaret never recovered. She died a few days later. With her last breath, she's reported to have whispered an apology to Edward for failing to give him a child to carry on his name."

"How sad!" Felicity said.

"Indeed. But there's more to the story. It was said that Lady Margaret's ghost continued to appear in Edward's house, looking for her baby. Servants claimed they saw her ghost gliding down the stairs carrying a lighted candle, or at the linen closet fetching a blanket to cover her child, or bending over the cradle intended for the baby. Edward claimed to feel her presence in the room where they used to sit in the evening, or to see her as a wavering light in their bed-chamber, where her possessions still rested on the dressing table."

Gooseflesh rose on the back of Felicity's neck. The tingling in her fingers—that couldn't have been Lady Margaret's presence . . . could it? No, it was silly to think that. She raised a hand to her neck and rubbed the gooseflesh away.

Ben had been listening intently to Father's

tale. "Is that why Sir Edward left England, to escape the ghost?"

"He did sail to America soon after his wife's death," Father replied. "But if he wanted to escape the ghost, he didn't succeed."

Felicity leaned forward. "The ghost followed him?"

"It seems Edward was unable to part with the items dear to the memory of his wife," Father said. "The brush and comb, rattle and cup went with him to the New World, and so did the ghost." Father's mouth had a quiver of mischief. "Even though Edward remarried and had other children, from whom both I and my cousin are descended, Lady Margaret continued to appear in whatever home housed her belongings. Or so the tale goes."

Felicity shivered. She liked to be scared—a little. But Father's story had left her feeling uneasy.

Ben chuckled. "Perhaps we'll have a visit from Lady Margaret tonight. Watch out, Lissie. She may come to your bedchamber and try to brush your long red tresses."

A Delivery

Felicity laughed, hoping she didn't sound as nervous as she felt. She heard Father going on, denying that there was truth to the ghost story. She knew he was right. She'd never believed in ghosts. Still, she couldn't shake off the odd sensation she'd had when she touched Lady Margaret's brush. She looked down at her hands and wiggled her fingers. They felt perfectly normal now.

Father's voice caught her attention. "Lissie, we must find a spot to display Lady Margaret's heirlooms until I'm able to sell them. Do you prefer the tilt-top table beside your mother's chair, or a shelf on the bookcase?" Father nodded toward the mahogany bookcase in the corner.

Locked up tight in the attic, was the thought that popped into Felicity's head. But she knew she was being silly. Of course the heirlooms should be set out where they could be seen and enjoyed. "I believe Mother would like them here on the table," Felicity said. "The sunlight shows them up nicely."

Father agreed. He asked Felicity to arrange the silver pieces on the table. Then he placed

Sir Edward's clock and pistols on the mantel, and Ben arranged the chessboard on the square gaming table near Father's desk. "Now," Father said to Ben, "we must be going. 'Tis nearly time to open the store. If we're not too busy today, I'll leave you in charge while I call on several gentlemen who may be interested in purchasing the heirlooms. Lady Margaret's silver pieces should be of great interest to them."

A razor-edged thought cut into Felicity's mind: *What if Lady Margaret is displeased at Father's plans to sell her belongings?*

2

MISTRESS OF THE HOUSE

Before Felicity had time to consider that uncomfortable idea, a knock sounded at the door. Felicity hurriedly finished arranging the heirlooms and went to answer the door.

A large, very plump woman stood on the doorstep. She wore a black linen dress with a black kerchief around her shoulders. A stiff white cap, grayed from many washings, covered her slate-gray hair. "Good morning to you," she said in a high-pitched voice. As she spoke, the fat on her neck quivered like jelly. "I'm looking for Mr. Merriman. Fetch him straightaway if you please, and be quick about it."

It was the rudest greeting Felicity had ever received, and she didn't know quite how to reply. "Of ... of course," Felicity stammered.

Then Father was beside Felicity, with his hand on her shoulder. "Mrs. Hewitt," he said in a firm voice. The woman nodded in acknowledgment, shaking her double chin. "I'm Mr. Merriman, and this is my daughter, Felicity."

"Oh, your daughter," Mrs. Hewitt said with a sniff. She turned to Felicity. "My apologies, miss. I mistook you for the serving girl."

"'Tis quite all right," Felicity said, though dread filled her. Must she endure two weeks of being treated in such a fashion?

"Do come in," Father said. Mrs. Hewitt stepped inside. Her sharp black eyes flicked past Father and Felicity to the tall clock in the hall, then to the mahogany side chairs and into the dining room, where Mother's silver tea service was visible on the sideboard.

"This way," Father said, extending his hand toward the parlor. Ben, minding his manners, stood up when Mrs. Hewitt came into the room, but he was frowning. Felicity could tell he didn't care for the woman either.

"This is my apprentice, Ben Davidson,"

Father said. "We were leaving to open my store just down the street."

"Yes, I know of Merriman's store," said Mrs. Hewitt. "I don't shop there myself. The prices are too dear for a poor widow woman like me."

Father raised an eyebrow. "Oh? I've been told our prices are among the best in Williamsburg."

"Perhaps," Mrs. Hewitt replied. "Truth be told, I shop infrequently. Since my dear husband's passing, poverty seems to be creeping upon me. Now, may I go to the kitchen? If I'm to serve dinner by one o'clock, as your wife requested, I should be getting to work. You recall, sir, that I must depart by mid-afternoon each day?"

Father said that he remembered. "My daughter will take you to the kitchen, Mrs. Hewitt." The kitchen was one of the outbuildings behind the main house. "Felicity will be able to answer any questions you have. We're off, then."

Ben and Father left. The door thudded shut behind them, and Felicity was alone with

Mrs. Hewitt. For a moment they stood looking at each other, and Mrs. Hewitt's black eyes seemed to bore through Felicity. Felicity struggled to think of something to say, but nothing would come to her. Why did she feel as if she were indeed the servant girl instead of the daughter of the house?

"Well, girl," Mrs. Hewitt said at last, "you have a fine home. But you understand that I'm to do no cleaning, do you not?"

Before Felicity could answer, Mrs. Hewitt began to strut about the room like an old hen, turning her head this way and that, her double chin bobbing. She touched Sir Edward's chess set and lingered at the mantel, admiring his clock. Then she turned, and her gaze fell on Lady Margaret's belongings. "Ah," she said, her eyes gleaming. "How very beautiful." She started toward the tilt-top table.

Felicity's anger flared. *That woman will not touch Lady Margaret's heirlooms.* Suddenly she felt brave. She stepped in front of Mrs. Hewitt. "I do understand you're to do no cleaning. My mother said you were here only to *help me* with the cooking."

Mrs. Hewitt's mouth twitched. "Oh, I'm to help *you*, am I?"

Felicity's heart pounded. She had to remember that *she* was running the household while Mother was gone, not Mrs. Hewitt. "Yes, ma'am," she said firmly.

Mrs. Hewitt looked down her nose at Felicity. "How old *are* you, miss? Nine? Ten?"

Felicity squared her shoulders. "I'm eleven."

Mrs. Hewitt snorted. "At your age, young miss, I was cooking in the Governor's Palace."

❧

The morning spent with Mrs. Hewitt in the kitchen seemed the longest of Felicity's life. The woman ordered Felicity about, criticizing everything she did—which made Felicity nervous, so she made one mistake after another. She spilled grease from the browning chicken into the fire, making the fire flare up and singe the chicken turning on a spit. She dropped a bowl of dried currants on the floor, cracking the wooden bowl and spilling currants everywhere. She shook too much pepper into the soup and grated too much ginger into the spice cake.

During dinner with Father and Ben, Felicity could scarcely eat because she dreaded cleaning up with Mrs. Hewitt. When Mrs. Hewitt finally left, Felicity breathed a sigh of relief. Yet she immediately began dreading tomorrow.

Felicity wanted to make Mother proud of the way she handled things in her absence. Here it was, though, not a day gone by, and Felicity already felt she had failed Mother miserably. It wasn't like Felicity to doubt herself or to lack confidence in her own ability. But how could *anyone* work well, she asked herself, with someone like Mrs. Hewitt waiting for her to trip up?

Felicity thought about the problem with Mrs. Hewitt while she worked in the garden that afternoon, picking the late peas and snap beans and digging turnips. Could she manage without

Mrs. Hewitt to help her with the cooking?
Felicity didn't think so. She was strong for an
eleven-year-old, but she could not lift the heavy
iron pots and the big brass kettle alone, nor chop
and haul all the wood for the fire, as well as haul
water and do all the cooking herself.

She needed *someone* to help her—but not
necessarily Mrs. Hewitt. Maybe Father could
let Mrs. Hewitt go and hire someone else. She
decided to talk to him about it that evening.

As it was, Father and Ben came home late
from the store, well after nightfall. Felicity had
kept supper warm, and the three of them ate in
the kitchen house. Father and Ben were dead
tired. The store had been bustling all day, and
the shelves had been nearly emptied. They'd
had to stay late and set out all the stock they
had left in the storeroom. "And still the shelves
look emptier than before the war," Ben commented.

Father looked so tired that Felicity hated to
burden him by talking about her problems with
Mrs. Hewitt. She had almost decided not to

mention it—maybe she could put up with the woman a little longer—when Father asked how her day had been. She hesitated; then she said, "Well enough, I suppose."

Father furrowed his brow. "Come now. I know my girl better than that. Something's bothering you, daughter. What is it?"

Felicity's troubles with Mrs. Hewitt poured out. When Felicity finished talking, Father didn't answer right away. So Ben piped up, "The woman gave *me* the cold shivers from the start. 'Tis no wonder that you found her hard to get along with."

"Perhaps Mrs. Hewitt's temperament is not the most agreeable," Father said. "But you'll have to do your best to work with her, Felicity. With so many people needed to help serve the travelers crowding the inns and taverns, it was difficult to find anyone who could come help us while your mother was away. Mrs. Hewitt was the only person available who could do the job. Yet she should know that she must treat you with the respect due the mistress of the house. For that is what you are until your mother returns. I'll speak to her about it in the morning."

Felicity nodded. A warm feeling was spreading over her. *The mistress of the house,* Father had called her. She would do her best to live up to his faith in her.

3
RACE DAY

The next morning when Mrs. Hewitt arrived,
Father ushered her into the parlor and closed the
door behind them. Felicity went into the kitchen
house and began preparations for the day's
meals. The horse races were to be that afternoon,
and Felicity wanted to be certain her chores
would be done in time to get Penny ready.

Felicity brought in wood from the woodpile
outside and rekindled a fire in the huge kitchen
fireplace. Then she hauled water from the well
so that she could put the coffeepot on to boil. As
she kneaded the bread dough she had set out last
night to rise, she stared out the open window
and daydreamed about what she would do with
the prize money if Penny won first place.

Felicity was so lost in her thoughts, she was

startled when Mrs. Hewitt whisked through the kitchen door. Without a word to Felicity, Mrs. Hewitt pulled out the Dutch oven and the bread pans and slammed them onto the grate over the fire to heat. She pulled out pots and rattled the lids so hard, the clatter echoed through Felicity's head. Felicity figured she was angry because Felicity had dared criticize her to Father.

It was like that all morning. Mrs. Hewitt scarcely spoke. Every now and then she would shoot Felicity a resentful glance, but Felicity pretended she didn't notice. Truthfully, she was glad she didn't have to listen to Mrs. Hewitt's complaints about how poor she was.

At last the midday meal was served, eaten, and cleared away, and Mrs. Hewitt went home. Felicity was finally free to get Penny groomed and saddled for the race. Ben had gone to the store to work a little longer; horses running in the afternoon race couldn't be signed in at the racetrack for more than an hour.

First Felicity went to her bedchamber and changed her clothes. She took her coral necklace out of the wooden box on her bureau. The necklace had belonged to Mother when she was a girl, and Felicity always wore it when she needed good luck.

As she started to put it on, she noticed that the clasp was coming loose. She debated whether she should wear the necklace; perhaps she should wait until it could go to the jeweler's to be repaired. She fiddled with the clasp. It seemed only slightly loose. "It should be all right," she told herself. "I'll be careful." She slipped the necklace around her neck and fastened it.

She went downstairs and out to the stable behind the house. Penny greeted Felicity with a nicker when she came in, and Felicity brushed her copper-colored coat until it shone. Penny's black foal, Patriot, kept nosing Felicity for attention and nudging at the pocket of her apron, where she often kept sugar lumps or carrots to give him.

"Sorry, fellow," Felicity said, laughing. "I've no treats for you today. You'll have to settle for oats." She got a few handfuls of oats from the feed bin and dumped them into a bucket to keep

RACE DAY

Patriot busy while she finished tending Penny. She cleaned Penny's hooves and combed out her mane and tail, all the while wondering what was keeping Ben. Surely an hour had passed by now.

When Felicity had wisped Penny's coat with a rope of twisted hay and still Ben hadn't come, anxiety began to stir inside her. If the store was very busy, maybe Ben wouldn't be able to get away in time for the race. And she couldn't go without him. Only men and boys were allowed to ride horses in the race.

She scolded herself. Ben would come if he could. If he didn't, there would be a good reason, and she would have to accept missing the race. She had dealt with worse disappointments. "Well," Felicity said to Penny, "I'll go ahead and get you saddled, so you'll be ready if Ben gets here."

She gave Penny an affectionate slap on the neck and went to the tack room to fetch Penny's saddle and saddle blanket. As she was reaching to pull a blanket off the shelf, she felt a nudge at her back. She whirled around. A whiskery

27

black nose pushed toward her and snuffled at her pocket, depositing bits of wet oats all over her apron. "Patriot!" Felicity cried. "How did you get in here? Did I leave the stall door open?"

Patriot's only answer was a loud snort, which sent more oats flying through the air, landing on Felicity's bodice. Felicity couldn't help smiling. "You rascal. Come on. Let's get you out of here."

She snatched a blanket and pushed Patriot out of the tack room and into the stall with Penny. Then she put the blanket on Penny's back and returned to the tack room to get the saddle, this time being careful to shut the stall door behind her. As she was cinching the girth of the saddle under Penny's belly, Ben came flying into the stable.

"Sorry I'm late," he said. "At the store I had to wait on a woman and her daughter who were trying to choose ribbons to match their ball gowns. I thought they would never make up their minds. Good thing you have Penny ready. We'll have to hurry to reach the course in time to sign Penny up for the race." The racetrack was half a mile outside of town, beyond the ivy-covered brick buildings of the College of William and Mary.

"You go on, Ben," Felicity said. "'Twill be much faster if you ride. I need to stop and pick up Elizabeth on the way. We'll meet you there."

Elizabeth lived a few blocks from Felicity, near the redbrick Governor's Palace, so graceful and solid behind its black iron gates. From the gates, the Palace green stretched in a broad avenue to Duke of Gloucester Street.

During the weeks of Publick Times, a fair took place on Market Square, just across from the green. Farmers and craftsmen set up stalls to sell their wares, and there were entertainments of all kinds: wrestling matches, juggling, plays, dancing, acrobats, and music. As Felicity hurried to Elizabeth's, Market Square was packed with people watching the festivities.

Elizabeth was waiting for Felicity on her front steps, her blonde hair neatly arranged under a starched white mob cap. She jumped up when she saw Felicity and met her at the gate. "I was

beginning to wonder if you'd forgotten me,"
Elizabeth said. She slipped through the gate to
join Felicity.

Felicity explained why she was late. "Let's
hurry. We want to have time to look over the
other horses before the race begins."

The girls made their way along the crowded
streets, past the college to the fields beyond.
Other people going to watch the races streamed
in the same direction. There were ladies and
gentlemen in traveling chairs, farmers and families in clattering carts, frontiersmen wearing
buckskins, Negro slaves and freedmen on foot,
and men and boys on horseback.

At last Felicity and Elizabeth arrived at the
racetrack, a wide path that made a circle a mile
long through the fields and woods. Beyond the
field lay dense forest, every leaf ablaze in autumn
tones of red and gold. Thick pines and sweet gum
trees grew at the forest's edge, and pinecones and
large, prickly burrs from the gum trees littered
the ground.

The horses that would run in the race were

standing near the starting line, some with heads bent to nibble grass. A short distance away were the booths where men could place bets on any horse they chose. Before the race began, the judges would assemble at the finish line to be ready to determine the winner. A single gunshot into the air would be the starting signal.

All over the field, people were standing in clumps. Some families were having picnics on the ground, and other people were buying food from vendors' stalls. There were men and women and children everywhere, dogs barking, horses neighing and snorting, people shouting, arguing, laughing, and talking.

Felicity and Elizabeth weaved through the crowd of people and horses, admiring sleek, elegant-limbed English horses and shaking their heads at long-backed, shaggy cart horses. "How could such homely horses ever hope to win a race?" Felicity wondered aloud.

Elizabeth reminded Felicity how ragged and rough Penny had looked before Felicity had freed her from her cruel owner, Jiggy Nye.

"No one would have guessed then that Penny could become as strong and beautiful as you've made her."

Felicity agreed. As they walked past, a boy about Ben's age who was standing beside a silvery-blue roan colt tipped his hat to Felicity and Elizabeth. The girls politely nodded back at him. The blue roan was about a year old and was being unruly—tossing his head, pinning back his ears, giving little bucks, and trying to kick.

When they were past him, Elizabeth said, "I wonder if that boy is entering his roan colt in the race."

"If he is," Felicity commented, "it looks as if the colt will give him a difficult time."

Then the girls spotted Ben and Penny and hurried over to them. Penny nickered at the sight of Felicity and put her face forward for Felicity to rub. Felicity stroked Penny while Ben explained how the race would work.

"Penny's heat will start soon," Ben said. "The best horses in each heat compete in the final race, and the winner of that race takes the prize purse.

All the horses waiting here will run in Penny's heat. From what I can tell, Penny stands a good chance to win, even if she is the only mare." Felicity knew mares could be at a disadvantage in a race because they tended not to be as muscular or as fast as males.

"Look them over for yourself," Ben recommended. "I want to place a wager on Penny." Then he hurried off to the betting stalls.

Felicity and Elizabeth patted Penny and studied the other horses. "What do you think?" Elizabeth asked. "Can Penny beat *all* these horses?"

Felicity gazed around. Most of the animals didn't seem to be much competition. They were not as well-built as Penny, or they were smaller or more unruly. Two, including the roan colt, were yearlings. There was a little quarter horse and a golden chestnut with legs as short as a pony's. An ugly piebald with big black spots was drooping his head to the ground as if he had no spirit at all.

The only animals that appeared as if they

would give Penny a good run were a gray gelding and a cream-colored stallion. Felicity noticed that the horses' owners, two gentlemen wearing riding boots, were staring at Penny. Both gentlemen were finely dressed, with well-made coats and breeches and snowy cravats at their necks.

When the men saw Felicity looking at their horses, they came over and introduced themselves as Mr. Minton and Mr. Yancey. Mr. Yancey was short and slight and had quick, intelligent eyes. The cream-colored stallion belonged to him. Mr. Minton was an older man with a pleasant, ruddy face. He owned the gray gelding.

"Please excuse us," said Mr. Minton. "My companion and I were discussing your mare. I'm certain I've seen her before. I believe she once belonged to a friend of mine, who owned a plantation on the York River near my own. I was with him when he purchased her for his granddaughter. I'd not easily forget such a beautiful animal."

Felicity's pulse quickened. "That was my grandfather." A wave of sadness rushed over her; Grandfather had died last winter.

Mr. Minton offered his condolences for her grandfather's death. He asked Felicity if he and Mr. Yancey could examine Penny more closely. "Of course," she said. The men began running their hands over Penny, admiring her sleek coat, her long, delicate legs, and her powerful haunches.

Suddenly there was a commotion a few yards away: frenzied barking and growling, the frightened whinny of a horse, shouting. Felicity and Elizabeth whirled and saw two dogs fighting and the dogs' owners trying to pull them apart. The unruly roan colt had reared at the noise, and the boy who had tipped his hat to the girls was trying to get the colt under control.

Then the disturbance was over, as quickly as it had begun. The dogs were separated, the colt calmed, and all the people who'd been watching the spectacle went back to their business. Felicity and Elizabeth returned their attention to Penny. Mr. Yancey and Mr. Minton had finished looking over Penny and were shaking their heads at the roan colt's behavior.

"No need to worry about that roan beating our horses," said Mr. Minton. "He's far too skittish. The lad there can scarcely control him. I doubt the roan will make it to the finish line."

"Hah," said Mr. Yancey. "He'll probably startle and toss the lad out of the saddle when the starting gun sounds." He turned to Felicity. "As for your horse, young miss, she looks very fast. But I don't think a mare has much chance of winning this race."

"Let's hope not, anyway," said Mr. Minton. "We've both wagered heavily on our own horses."

"And I intend to wager more heavily," said Mr. Yancey. "Come, Minton. We've time yet before the race to get to the betting booth."

Before Felicity could say that she thought Penny had a very good chance of winning, even if she *was* a mare, the two men had hurried away.

4

The Boy with the Roan Colt

Felicity flung her arm around Penny's neck. "Don't worry, girl," she said, her cheek against the hollow of Penny's shoulder. "Those men don't know everything. You've got more spirit than all the other horses put together."

"Yes," said Elizabeth, rubbing Penny's velvety nose. "And that's what it takes to win at anything. Not just being a boy or a girl." Penny's ears swiveled forward as if she understood.

"Aye. I agree to that for sure." The voice came from beyond Penny, on the opposite side.

Felicity ducked under Penny's neck to see who was speaking. It was the boy they'd seen with the roan yearling. His face was tanned and his hair, tied behind his neck, was golden brown. He looked as if he'd spent a lot of time in the sun. Felicity glanced over at the roan a few yards away. The colt was perfectly calm now, munching contentedly out of a feedbag. She was impressed at how quickly the boy had soothed his horse.

"Good day to ye both," the boy said. "Lovely mare you've got. Will she be running next?"

At least that's what Felicity *thought* the boy had said. He spoke in an accent so thick, she wasn't sure she had understood him.

Elizabeth must have understood him, for she answered quickly, "Yes, Penny is entered in the next heat." Then she asked, "Are you from Yorkshire, in England? Your speech sounds as if you are. My family comes from near there, in Lancashire."

"I'm from wherever I am at the moment," the boy said with a friendly smile. "Is the mare yours then, miss?"

"Penny isn't mine," Elizabeth replied. "She belongs to my friend here, Felicity. And my name is Elizabeth."

"'Tis a pleasure to meet you both," he said, sweeping off his tricornered hat. "I'm Dawson.

A pity your horse is in the next heat. I was going to ask if you needed a jockey, but I've already been hired for that heat."

"You're riding the roan yearling, aren't you?" Felicity asked. Her voice was full of admiration. The boy was obviously a skilled horseman.

"He's rather wild," Elizabeth commented.

Dawson grinned. "Spirited is all. The lady who's paying me to race him for her says he's fast as the wind and sure to place first, if I can stay in the saddle. Both she and her husband are scared to ride him. Seems he threw one of their grooms and broke the man's neck."

Elizabeth's eyes went wide. "Doesn't that frighten you?"

Dawson drew back his shoulders in pride. "Not at all. I was riding before I could walk. My father was head groom on a huge estate in England, and he taught me all he knew."

"What did he teach you?" Felicity asked. She was always eager to learn more about horses.

"Just about everything," Dawson said with a swagger. "How to read a horse like a book.

How to recognize the best horses, such as this lass here." He let Penny sniff his hand, and then he stroked her neck. "What a grand mare! She'll likely beat every horse here, even my roan. A shame, too. I was to be paid double if the roan won. Still, there's always a chance . . ."

At that moment Ben walked up. "A chance of what?" he asked, looking at Dawson. "I don't think we've met."

Felicity introduced Ben to Dawson and told Ben that Dawson was riding the roan yearling in the race. Briefly the boys talked about horses. Ben asked Dawson if he had bet any money on the roan.

"What money?" said Dawson. "I'm down to my last shilling. Couldn't have eaten tonight if I hadn't been hired to ride in the race. I need to find a job, but I'm new to town and don't know where to look."

"I may know of a job for you," Ben said. Absently he scratched Penny's muzzle. "At least a temporary one, in the store where I'm an apprentice. Mr. Merriman, Felicity's father, was saying this morning that he needs extra help during Publick Times. Why don't you come by the store tomorrow?"

Ben told Dawson how to find the store. Then Dawson gave Penny a gentle slap and went back to tend the roan.

A crowd had begun to gather at the starting line, and some of the people walked over to Penny. Word had gotten around that Penny was the only mare in the heat, and they wanted to see her more closely. Mr. Yancey came back to tell Felicity that he'd placed a small wager on Penny.

"Against your own horse?" Felicity said.

Mr. Yancey managed a smile. "I don't look at it that way. I think of it more as increasing my odds of winning." He scratched Penny between the ears.

People were milling around Penny and making her nervous. She was snorting, flicking her ears, and stamping her feet. Felicity tried to calm her, but it didn't work. There were too many strangers nearby, and they were talking too loudly and asking Felicity, Ben, and Elizabeth too many questions. Felicity turned her head from side to side, trying to watch Penny and to answer questions, until she felt dizzy. It made her uneasy to have so many strangers putting their hands on Penny, but she didn't know how to ask them not to touch her horse without seeming to be rude.

Finally everyone drifted away from Penny, back toward the starting post. Horses were beginning to line up for the race. Mr. Yancey shook Ben's hand. "May the best horse win," he said as he left them.

"Must be almost time for the starting gun," said Ben. "Lissie, you and Elizabeth should find a place to watch. There's a grassy rise beyond the betting stalls where you can see most of the track. It has a good view of the finish line as well. Better hurry."

Felicity planted a kiss on Penny's nose, and Penny's soft lips ran over Felicity's face. "Do your best, my pretty girl," said Felicity. She touched her hand to her coral necklace. "And good luck." As she and Elizabeth left, Ben was mounting

Penny and heading to the starting post.

When Felicity and Elizabeth reached the grassy rise, it was filling up with people. People were sitting on boulders and tree stumps and standing anywhere they could find an open spot. The girls tried to squeeze through the crowd to the edge of the hill where they could see, but their view was always blocked by taller people in front of them.

Frustrated, Felicity said, "We won't be able to see a thing!"

"I know," said Elizabeth. "Just our fortune to be stuck behind the man with the largest wig and the woman with the largest bonnet!"

"Come over here!" A freckle-faced girl in an oversized mob cap and worn homespun dress was beckoning to them. She was perched on a rocky outcrop that jutted from the side of the hill; below, the rise sloped sharply down. Felicity and Elizabeth waved their thanks and hurried over.

The girl told them her name was Anne, and Felicity and Elizabeth introduced themselves to her. When they stood with her on the rocks, they could see most of the racetrack, though a grove of trees obscured the starting line. In the distance, the rooftops of Williamsburg showed through gaps in the autumn foliage.

Felicity's stomach fluttered. How she wished she could see Ben and Penny at the starting post! She was worried because Penny had never raced before.

"Penny will be fine," Elizabeth reassured her. "You know how Penny loves to run."

"My guardian has a horse in the race, too," Anne said. Then she touched a finger to Felicity's hair. "It isn't often I meet anyone with hair as red as mine."

Felicity looked sharply at Anne. Now she noticed that Anne did indeed have curly red hair, though it was almost buried under her mob cap. "Many people in my family have red hair," Felicity said. She told Anne and Elizabeth about Lady Margaret's long red tresses and the silver vanity set Felicity's father had inherited.

"It would be nice to know so much about your family," said Anne. "I don't know anything

44

about mine. My mama and papa died when I was four years old. I've lived with my guardian and his wife ever since, but they aren't related to me."

"You must think of them as your family by now," Elizabeth commented.

Anne shrugged. "I don't know. I do all their cooking and cleaning and try my best, but they never seem happy with me."

Felicity felt sorry for Anne. Felicity had been worried about the responsibility of keeping house alone for two weeks, but Anne had to do it all the time—and for people who sounded as impossible to please as Mrs. Hewitt.

"I know how you feel!" Felicity blurted out. "Well, at least a little." She told Anne about Mother going away and leaving Felicity in charge of the household. "It feels so strange being alone in that big house."

Anne's eyes were bright with interest. "Where do you live?"

"On Duke of Gloucester Street," Felicity answered. "A block and a half from Merriman's store, if you know where that is."

"The store belongs to Felicity's father," Elizabeth threw in.

"Yes," Anne said. "I believe I've seen it."

Anne looked ready to ask a question, but at that moment came the *boom* of the starting gun. The horses were off!

Excitement hummed through the crowd. People pressed in closer and closer to the rocky area where the girls were standing until shoulders were touching shoulders. Yet no one could see where the horses were on the track because of the trees. People were jostling and pushing, trying to get a better view.

From beyond the trees came hoots and cheers from spectators near the starting line. Felicity heard the pounding of hooves, but she couldn't see anything. She leaned forward, straining to snatch a glimpse through the trees of horses and riders.

Then someone—she didn't know who—bumped against her, and she lost her balance. Anne and Elizabeth each grabbed one of her hands and kept her from falling.

At the same time, the horses came bursting from behind the trees. Felicity heard the roar of the crowd, the thunder of the horses barreling up the track. In a flash the horses were sweeping past. Penny was in the lead, next was the cream-colored stallion, and then the gray gelding. Yards behind were the other horses, all in a pack.

Something was wrong, though, with Penny. Felicity could tell, even from this distance. Penny's strides were uneven. Her head was not thrust forward, with her nose up to the wind, as she usually ran. Instead she held her nose down as if she was in pain, and she was tossing her head as if trying to rid herself of the bit.

Then the unthinkable happened. Penny broke stride and stumbled. Felicity's knees went weak.

Was Penny going to go down?

5

SHADOWS AT DUSK

The next seconds stretched into eternity.
The horses seemed to move in the horrible slow
action of dreams. For a moment, Felicity thought
Penny would collapse and fall underneath the
fury of sharp, flying hooves.

Then Penny was up again, her footing re-
gained. In that short time, though, both the
cream stallion and the gray gelding had passed
her. Their legs stretched out, leaving Penny
behind. Mr. Minton on the gray was gaining
steadily on Mr. Yancey's stallion.

Felicity kept her eyes fastened on Penny.
Penny was running, but her heart wasn't in it.
Ben was standing in the saddle, leaning low
over Penny's shoulder, urging her on, but Penny
kept falling farther behind the gelding and the

stallion. Little by little the other horses passed her, too—first the roan yearling, then the little quarter horse, the piebald, the other yearling, and the golden chestnut. Penny finished the race in last place.

Felicity felt sick with fear and disappointment. Elizabeth clutched Felicity's hand, her eyes betraying her own fear. "What's wrong with Penny, Felicity?"

Felicity gulped back tears. "Let's go see."

People were already surging toward the finish line, so Felicity and Elizabeth pushed their way into the flow of people. It occurred to Felicity that Anne had disappeared sometime during the race. Felicity had been so worried about Penny, she hadn't even noticed. Fleetingly, Felicity wondered which horse had belonged to Anne's guardian. Neither she nor Elizabeth had thought to ask.

Felicity and Elizabeth struggled through the confusion of people and horses at the finish line, looking for Penny and Ben. Out of the corner of her eye, Felicity caught sight of Mr. Minton and his gray surrounded by well-wishers. His gray must have won the race, but all Felicity cared about now was finding Penny. Finally she saw Penny and Ben. Ben, his face streaked with dirt, was dismounting Penny. Rivulets of sweat ran down Penny's heaving sides. Felicity dashed up to Penny and cradled Penny's head between her hands. Penny gazed back at Felicity, her large liquid eyes so full of pain, it wrenched Felicity's heart.

Ben was kneeling beside Penny, running his hands over her legs. "What happened, Ben?" Felicity said. "Did she go lame?"

"We've been so worried about her!" Elizabeth said.

Ben straightened, his brow furrowed with concern. "She doesn't appear to be lame. Whatever happened to her was gradual. When the race started, she was fine. She jumped into the lead, but around the first bend she began to slow up and to miss strides."

"We saw her stumble," said Felicity, stroking Penny's muzzle.

Ben nodded grimly. "Yet I can't find anything wrong with her."

"Could she be sick?" Elizabeth asked.

"She must be," Felicity said. She stepped around to Penny's side. "Let's get this girth loosened, Ben, and get her home."

Bracing herself with a hand on the saddle blanket, Felicity bent to loosen the girth around Penny's belly. Penny jerked and swung her neck toward Felicity, her ears laid flat and a dangerous glint in her eye. Felicity drew back, shocked at Penny's reaction.

"What'd you do to her, Felicity?" Ben asked.

"Nothing!" Felicity said. "But I felt a lump under the blanket. That's what seemed to set her off."

"Let's unsaddle her," said Ben. He loosened the girth strap and lifted off the saddle. Felicity pulled away the blanket underneath and gasped at what she saw: several large, prickly burrs from a sweet gum tree had been lodged under the blanket and had made raw sores on Penny's back.

"Oh, Ben." Tears gathered at the corners of

Felicity's eyes. "These burrs must have been biting into Penny from the moment you mounted, until she couldn't stand it any longer." As Felicity gently picked the burrs from Penny's sweaty hide, Penny grunted with pain. Felicity flung the hateful burrs on the ground.

Elizabeth was staring in disbelief. "How did sweet gum burrs get under Penny's blanket?"

"That's what I want to know," Ben said. "Were they stuck on the blanket when you saddled her?"

"Of course not!" Felicity said hotly. Even as she spoke, a picture rushed into her mind: Patriot poking his nose into the tack room and distracting her as she was getting a blanket for Penny. Had she accidentally grabbed a dirty blanket?

Guilt shot through her. Why hadn't she paid closer attention to what she was doing?

"I'm sorry, Lissie," Ben was saying. "I know how careful you are with Penny's equipment. It's just that these sores could cause serious problems if they don't heal properly." Ben looked anguished. "And I kept urging her to run when

I knew something was wrong. If the sores cause trouble for Penny, it'll be my fault!"

"Mine, too," said Felicity. She told Ben and Elizabeth about the mistake she might have made with the blanket. An echo of Mother's voice sounded in Felicity's ears: *Pay attention to the task at hand . . . pay attention . . .*

Felicity clenched her fists, furious with herself. "Why wasn't I more careful?"

Elizabeth laid a hand on Felicity's arm. "What's done is done," she said gently. "It isn't any help to Penny for the two of you to stand around blaming yourselves."

"Elizabeth's right," said Ben. "We need to get Penny home and clean these sores. I'll take her. Lissie, you and Elizabeth go by the apothecary's shop on Prince George Street and get some powdered willow bark."

"I know the place," Elizabeth said. "It's down the street from my house."

"It's right on your way," said Ben. "Willow bark in Penny's oats will ease her pain. You'll have to ask the apothecary to charge the medicine to your father's account. I wagered all my money on Penny winning the race. I thought it was a sure bet."

Felicity knew Father wouldn't be happy if he knew Ben had gambled his money away, but she couldn't really blame Ben. They had all been so certain Penny would win.

❦

Elizabeth went with Felicity to the apothecary's shop. After they'd purchased the willow bark, Elizabeth said she had to go home. "I hope Penny will be all right," she said. "Please come by tomorrow and let me know." Felicity promised.

With worry over Penny sharp in her mind, Felicity started home across Market Square. The square was bathed in the slanting light of late afternoon, and its lush grass was scattered with patches of mud churned up by the day's fair-goers. The crowd from the fair was beginning to dwindle, but lots of people were still walking around, shopping at stalls, or watching the entertainment.

Shrill voices and laughter came from a roped-off area in the middle of the square where there was a soaped-pig-catching contest. Nearby was a man playing a fiddle and dancing a jig. Some distance away, in front of a curtained stage, a cluster of people were watching a puppet show. At the back of the audience, Felicity spotted Anne. It was hard to miss Anne's oversized mob cap.

As Felicity watched, Anne stumbled into a wealthy-looking woman who was wearing a fancy bonnet with lace draped around the brim. When Anne clutched the woman's arm to keep them both from falling, the woman's bonnet tumbled off her head into a mud puddle.

Anne said something to the woman that Felicity couldn't hear. The woman, in a rage, started yelling at Anne. Felicity could hear every word. "You clumsy girl! You've ruined my best bonnet. You'll pay for it, I do declare." The woman raised her umbrella and shook it in Anne's face. "Where is your father? You'll take me to him at once if you know what's good for you."

Anne shrank back from the woman. Even though Anne looked small and scared, no one made a move to come to her aid. For a split second, Felicity considered whether she should try to help Anne. Was there even anything she could do? She needed to get home quickly to get the willow bark to Penny, but she couldn't leave Anne to face that woman's anger alone. Felicity hurried toward Anne, calling out to her.

Anne turned, and for a moment their eyes met. Then Felicity blinked, and Anne was gone, swallowed up by the crowd. Felicity's eyes roved among the knots of people on the square in search of Anne's distinctive mob cap, but Anne had disappeared—again.

Felicity couldn't understand it. Had Anne not recognized her? At least Anne had gotten away from that disagreeable woman, Felicity thought.

She turned around and cut across Market Square to her own street. Dusk was beginning to fall. The red roof of the capitol building, on the east end of town, glowed from the setting sun. As Felicity walked home, candlelight was already winking from some of the windows.

The day had been warm for October, but with evening approaching, a chill wind had set in. People were hurrying to their destinations. Brittle fallen leaves, driven by the wind, rattled across the street and swirled in furious circles in Felicity's path. She had walked this way a hundred times, but tonight, for some reason, she felt ill at ease, as if someone was following her. She thought of stories she'd heard of robberies during Publick Times, and a shiver ran down her spine.

Was there someone behind her, waiting until she was alone on the street to rob her?

6
A Light in the Parlor

Quickly she spun around. No one was there.
A lone man on horseback clopped past in the
street, going in the other direction. Nothing
moved in the shadowed yards behind the picket
fences that lined the sidewalks. A few doors
down, two women, talking and laughing, came
out of a shop, turned the corner, and vanished
from sight.

Felicity released the breath she'd been holding. *I'm being silly*, Felicity told herself. *Who would
want to rob a girl my age?* She was almost home
anyway, only two blocks more.

She picked up her pace, hurrying past a gun-
smith's shop and the candle maker's. Finally she
was at her own front gate. She went through, and
the gate clicked shut behind her. "Home," she

whispered to herself. *Safe,* she added silently.

She headed down the path and around back to the stable. Penny was in her stall with Patriot, munching hay. Ben had washed Penny's sores, and she already seemed calmer. Felicity gave Ben the powdered willow bark, and he mixed it into a hot bran mash for Penny. Penny gobbled the mash hungrily.

"Well," Felicity said with a thin smile, "everything she's been through today doesn't seem to have affected her appetite."

"A healthy appetite is a good sign," Ben said. "By tomorrow we should know whether or not the sores will cause trouble for her. The willow bark will help her get a good night's sleep."

Later, Felicity prepared a simple supper of smoked fish, cheese, and pickled vegetables. When Father came home, they all ate in the kitchen, and Felicity and Ben told Father about Penny. "We can hope she'll be better by morning," Father said. Felicity was in an exhausted daze as she cleaned up the supper things and mixed dough for tomorrow's bread. After she had set out the dough to rise and banked the fire, she locked the kitchen house and went to bed.

In her bedchamber, she took off her dress, unlaced her stays, and put everything away in the clothes press. Then she realized her coral necklace was missing. She searched for it in the folds of the clothes she'd taken off, on the floor, under the dressing table, even under the rug. But she didn't find it.

Felicity had a sinking feeling in her chest. "I must have lost it at the racetrack," she told herself. "Or on the way home." The last time she remembered having the necklace was before the race, when she'd touched it for good luck.

She slumped to the bed. "It could be any-where. I'll probably never find it." She shouldn't have worn the necklace until the clasp had been repaired. What would Mother say when she found out the necklace was gone?

Feeling miserable, Felicity climbed into bed. She was angry with herself. Why couldn't she learn to be more careful? Mother was always scolding her about it. Felicity's carelessness had cost her the coral necklace, and it might have been the cause of Penny getting those terrible sores. She wondered how much the sores were hurting Penny, and whether Penny would be better in the morning . . . or worse.

Felicity started thinking hard about Penny. She was *certain* that the blanket hadn't had burrs in it when she saddled Penny. Even if Felicity hadn't noticed burrs when she grabbed the blanket from the tack room, she was sure that she would've seen or felt the burrs while she was saddling Penny.

Besides, how could sweet gum burrs have gotten stuck in the blanket unless it had been lying on the ground under a sweet gum tree? *And we don't have any sweet gum trees on our property,* she realized.

"It couldn't have been my fault," Felicity said, springing up to a sitting position. "It *wasn't* my fault."

Then how had the burrs gotten into Penny's blanket?

Felicity tossed off the covers and swung

her legs over the side of the bed. She knew she wouldn't be able to sleep—not until she figured this out.

She slipped out of bed, went to the window, opened it, and leaned out. She stared out over the sleeping town, the dark roofs and treetops. Smoke-gray clouds drifted across a bright full moon. She could almost see to Market Square. Its edges were framed by lanterns gleaming from the Palace cupola on one end and the courthouse on the other.

Suddenly something occurred to her: beside the courthouse was a grove of sweet gum trees. Every fall, sweet gum burrs covered the ground there and littered the sidewalk and the street in front of the courthouse. Ben would have ridden Penny underneath the trees on his way to the racetrack. Could burrs have fallen off the trees onto Penny and somehow worked themselves underneath the blanket?

No, it was too unlikely an explanation. The burrs had been wedged far back underneath the blanket *and* the saddle. Either the burrs had been caught in the blanket before Penny was saddled—or they had been *pushed* under the saddle and blanket on purpose.

Felicity stood up straight so fast that she nearly hit her head on the window sash. Her heart was pounding. Had someone done just that? Purposely put burrs under Penny's blanket to keep her from winning the race?

Felicity started pacing the room. So many people had come by to admire Penny before the race. Any one of them could have done it. But who would have been so cruel?

She tried to recall all the people who had stopped to look at Penny, but their names and faces ran together. The only ones she could remember were Dawson, Mr. Yancey, and Mr. Minton. Dawson had said he would be paid double if the roan colt won. And Mr. Yancey and Mr. Minton had lots of money at stake from the bets they had placed on their own horses. Had one of them done it?

Dawson was so pleasant and friendly, Felicity couldn't imagine him doing such a thing. But he had said that he needed work and was down to his last few shillings. Would he have hurt Penny in order to earn enough money to live?

Mr. Yancey and Mr. Minton seemed to be gentlemen and genuine horse lovers. Mr. Yancey had wagered on Penny himself, so he would have benefited even if Penny had won. And Felicity couldn't believe that anyone who had been a friend of Grandfather, as Mr. Minton had, could have purposely hurt a horse. Yet Mr. Minton's horse *had* won the race. Did winning mean enough to him that he would have harmed Penny to do it?

Felicity's thoughts went back and forth, in and out, until they were all tangled up in knots. On top of that, she was worried about Penny. How was Penny doing? Was her back still hurting? Were the sores getting worse?

Not knowing is worse than knowing, Felicity thought. She couldn't stay in her chamber another second. She had to go out to the stable and check on Penny.

She pulled on her dressing gown and slippers

and opened her door. Not a sound came from Father's bedchamber or anywhere else in the house. Felicity crept to the stairs and started down; then she stopped dead, the skin on the back of her neck prickling at what she saw. The parlor's double doors were partly open, and through the crack came a glowing light.

One thing jumped into Felicity's mind: *Lady Margaret's ghost.*

Felicity stood still, gripping the banister. "I don't believe in ghosts," she whispered. But her heart was thudding. She made herself move down the remaining stairs, then across the hall's polished floor to the parlor doors. Scarcely daring to breathe, she put a hand to the doorknob and peered inside. The parlor was wrapped in an eerie, wavering light that cast an unnatural sheen on Lady Margaret's heirlooms.

For a second Felicity fought against terror. But as she watched, the light shrank to a sliver shining from the window, faded, and was gone. *The moon*, Felicity thought with sudden understanding. *It was only the moon through the broken shutter. And now the clouds have covered the moon.*

She felt foolish. How could she have allowed her imagination to run away with her so? She turned and headed through the house to go to the stable. She let out the latch on the back door and went down the stone steps to the path that led to the outbuildings.

As she passed through the dark yard, she shivered, but not from the chill. For the second time that evening, she had the distinct feeling that someone was watching her.

She scanned the dark, shadowy yard. Nothing stirred. Above her, a breeze rustled through the apple trees loaded with fruit. The moon slid out from behind the clouds and frosted the scene in silver light. Still Felicity saw nothing unusual.

You can't see a ghost.

The thought popped into her mind before Felicity could stop it. Quickly she pushed the thought away. "What's gotten into me tonight?" she murmured. With an impatient sigh, she hurried on to the stable.

She found Penny and Patriot sleeping in

their stall. Penny was breathing evenly, and Patriot was making snuffling noises in his sleep. Felicity smiled at the two horses, sleeping so soundly. "Get well, my girl," she whispered.

Felicity slipped out of the stable and started toward the house. Her mind returned to puzzling over the burrs. As she walked between the smokehouse and the kitchen, out of the corner of her eye she caught a flash of white—there one moment, gone the next.

Felicity caught her breath. *The ghost!*

7
DAWSON'S REMEDY

Terror-stricken, Felicity sprinted for the back door and flew into the house. Not daring to look into the parlor, she raced up the stairs and into her own chamber. She shut the door behind her, leaped into bed with her dressing gown still on, and pulled the covers up to her chin.

Her breath came fast and hard, and her pulse beat in her throat. She half-expected to see the door open and the ghost of Lady Margaret come floating into the bedchamber. After a few minutes, when nothing happened, Felicity's breathing slowed. She began to feel very foolish.

That flash of white in the yard had probably been nothing more than some bird flushed from its roost, or an owl or a startled rabbit. Why hadn't she gone to investigate instead of dashing for the house like a superstitious little girl?

Maybe she was just that—a little girl. Maybe Mother had been wrong to think that Felicity was a young woman who could handle the responsibility of a household. She certainly hadn't done a very good job so far.

"I'll do better, starting tomorrow," Felicity said. She wouldn't let Father's ghost stories frighten her again. With that promise to herself, she fell asleep.

🐉

The morning didn't start as well as Felicity had hoped. First, she overslept.

She didn't wake up until she heard Mrs. Hewitt knocking on the front door and Father letting her in. By the time Felicity had dressed and gotten to the bottom of the stairs, she heard Mrs. Hewitt in the back hallway telling Father that she'd discovered the Merrimans' back door was unlatched.

Felicity's heart gave a lurch. She had forgotten

to fasten the latch when she ran into the house last night! Of all people to discover her mistake, why did it have to be Mrs. Hewitt?

"'Tis a dangerous thing, sir," Mrs. Hewitt was saying, "with so many strangers in town for Publick Times, to leave a door unfastened overnight."

"Perhaps you're mistaken," Father replied. "I pulled in the back-door latch myself before I went up to my chamber last night."

Mrs. Hewitt clucked. "All I know, sir, is what I know. 'Twas unfastened when I started for the kitchen a moment ago. Come see for yourself, if you please."

Felicity knew she had to come forward and admit what she had done. Swallowing hard, she stepped out into the hall where Father and Mrs. Hewitt could see her. "Father," Felicity said, "'twas I who left the door unfastened. I went outside to check on Penny last night, and I must have forgotten to pull in the latch when I came back."

Father gave an exasperated sigh. "I don't have to tell you, Felicity, how careless that was. And neither should I have to remind you not to leave this house after dark without my knowledge, even if it's only to go to the stable."

Her cheeks flaming, Felicity promised Father she wouldn't let it happen again. She didn't miss the satisfied smirk on Mrs. Hewitt's face.

Preparing breakfast with Mrs. Hewitt was torture for Felicity. The woman was even worse at faultfinding and acted even more superior than usual, and Felicity couldn't seem to make an effort at taking charge herself. All she wanted to do was rush through her tasks in the kitchen so that she could go check on Penny.

At last the meal was served and the cleanup finished. Father and Ben went to the store. Felicity made an excuse to Mrs. Hewitt and escaped to the stable.

As soon as Felicity entered the stable, she knew something was wrong. Penny was pacing her stall. Back and forth Penny went, back and forth, snorting, tossing her head, and frantically flicking her tail, as if trying to rid herself of a swarm of biting flies. Patriot, not understanding what was wrong with his mother, was watching her with wide eyes and flaring nostrils.

Felicity's stomach knotted. Had wishful thinking made her too eager to believe last night that Penny's sores weren't going to give her any trouble? Felicity went to the stall's half door and called for Penny, but she wouldn't come. Now that Felicity was closer, she saw the reason for Penny's distress: the sores on her back had become open patches of flesh, oozing yellow pus and blood. Penny kept thrusting her head around, trying to bite at the sores. She must be wild with pain.

Something had to be done to help Penny, and quickly, but Felicity had no idea what. She needed Father's help. Without bothering to tell Mrs. Hewitt she was leaving, Felicity took off for the store.

Duke of Gloucester Street had never seemed so long. Once Felicity was in sight of the store's painted sign, she ran the rest of the way. Lifting her skirts, she took the front stairs two at a time. The door was open to the warm morning, and Felicity could hear Father and Ben talking to someone. She peered inside. It was Dawson. She didn't see any other customers. Ben was telling Father about meeting Dawson at the race. "He needs a job, and you were saying, sir, that you could use some extra help during Publick Times."

Felicity burst into the store. "Father! Penny's much worse, and she's in terrible pain!" A sob caught in her throat. "I'm afraid for her!"

Ben slammed his palm on the counter. "I should have checked on Penny this morning! She was doing so well last night, I thought she was going to be fine."

"It isn't your fault, Ben," Felicity choked out. "She's my horse; I'm responsible for her."

Father hurried around the counter and laid a comforting hand on Felicity's shoulder. "Calm down, Lissie, and tell me exactly what's wrong with her."

Felicity described the festering sores. Dawson spoke up. "I think I know how to cure Penny. My father owned a stable in London, and he used a special salve on such wounds. It worked wonders, and very quickly, too."

Something he said nudged at the back of Felicity's mind, but she ignored it. "Could you make some of the salve for Penny?" she asked.

"If I had the right ingredients, I could," Dawson promised.

"If you can cure Penny with your salve," said Father, "I'll give you a job for as long as you need it." He asked Dawson what ingredients he needed for the salve and Dawson told him.

"We have all those here at the store," Father said. Father had Ben gather the ingredients from the shelves, and then he sent Ben off with Felicity and Dawson to tend to Penny.

The three of them hurried along the crowded walk, scarcely speaking a word. They had to dodge a running boy rolling a hoop and slaves loading a wagon with bricks. A carriage clattered past, and militiamen trotted by on horseback. Up ahead in front of a tavern, two sailors were engaged in a loud argument.

Dawson gave the sailors a worried glance. "Quick, let's cross the street," he said. "Those fellows look as if they're about to come to blows."

He was already into the street before Ben or Felicity could say anything.

They followed him across the street, but he was walking so fast, they didn't catch up with him until they were well past the tavern. Then he stopped and turned to Felicity with a sheepish grin. "I was in such a hurry to get to your house, I forgot I don't know where you live."

Felicity had to catch her breath before she could answer. "'Tis there." She pointed down the street to her white clapboard house but shot a puzzled glance at Dawson. "I was afraid you were going to go past it. Why didn't you wait for us, Dawson?"

"Worried about Penny is all," Dawson said. "Is the stable in back?"

"Yes," Ben said. "I'll show you." Ben and Dawson headed toward the house. Felicity followed.

When they got to the stable, Penny was still pacing. Felicity eased into the stall and crooned to her, while Ben and Dawson mixed the salve. After Felicity had Penny calmed, Dawson slowly entered the stall and let Penny sniff his hand. As Felicity and Ben held Penny's halter, Dawson smoothed the salve over Penny's back, all the while talking quietly to her.

Watching Dawson's gentle way with Penny, Felicity wondered how she could have suspected him of putting the burrs under Penny's saddle. He was far too kind and caring, she thought, to have tried to harm Penny in order to win a race.

Once Dawson had covered all the sores, Penny seemed herself again. Felicity couldn't believe how well the salve worked. "Dawson," she said, "you've worked a miracle."

"I have to agree," said Ben.

"Penny feels better for now," Dawson said, "because of the soothing ingredients in the salve. But it has to be applied every few hours for several days before the sores will truly begin to heal. Someone will have to stay with her all night to put it on."

"Could you do it, Dawson?" Felicity asked. "I know Father would let you sleep here in the stable and take meals with us, if you're willing."

Dawson shot Ben a questioning glance. "Do you think Mr. Merriman would be agreeable to that?"

"I know he would," said Ben.

Dawson grinned. "'Twould beat sleeping in alleys and haystacks, to be sure."

"You've been sleeping outside?" Felicity asked. The days in October were often warm, but the nights were chilly. "Why, Dawson?"

"No money, no choices," he said lightly. "A fellow's got to eat, but a bed you can do without."

For a moment neither Felicity nor Ben said anything. Felicity was thinking how she'd always taken for granted that she would have food to eat and a roof over her head. She was sure Ben was thinking the same thing.

"What brought you to Williamsburg in the first place?" Ben asked.

With no money and no job, Felicity added silently.

Dawson shrugged. "One thing and another." He turned to Felicity. "Tell me, how did Penny get those nasty sores on her back?"

Felicity and Ben told him about the burrs and how Penny had floundered in the race because she was in such pain.

"That explains her poor finish," Dawson said. "I'd been puzzled about that. It isn't often I'm mistaken about a horse's abilities." Then he wrinkled his brow. "I just wonder..."

"What?" Felicity asked.

"It could be only a coincidence, but I saw something very odd the day of the race, when I was getting the roan colt ready to run. 'Twas just before the heat was to begin, y'know." He told them that he had spotted a girl at the edge of the woods gathering sweet gum burrs in her apron. Thinking it was strange to be gathering common burrs as if they were nuts, he had asked her what she was doing. "She told me that her guardian had sent her out to get him some burrs and warned her to be quick about it. Then she shuddered, as if she was scared of the man, and said, 'He ain't the kind of man who likes to be questioned.'

"I felt sorry for her," he added. "She was

such a little thing, her mob cap nearly covered her whole face—"

"What did you say?" Felicity cut in.

"I said her cap covered her face—"

"Did she have red hair?" Felicity demanded.

"Yes, as a matter of fact, she did," Dawson replied.

"Anne!" Felicity exclaimed. "It must have been her!" Quickly she explained to Ben and Dawson who Anne was. "And her guardian had a horse in the race, too. He must have been one of the people who came by to admire Penny, and he wanted to hurt Penny's chances of winning the race. But it's hard to believe that Anne would have helped him do it."

"Maybe she didn't have any choice," Dawson began.

"How could she not have a choice?" Felicity said angrily. "Nobody forced her to gather those burrs."

"I'm not so sure about that," Dawson said. "The girl had her sleeves pulled up, and I saw bruises on her arms. Her guardian has been mistreating her, I think, and probably forcing her to steal for him, too." He went on to tell Felicity and Ben how the girl had tried to pick his pocket. "She came over to look at the roan and pretended to bump into me. I caught her trying to slide my money purse out of my pocket. She was slick, all right. She was so good that an ordinary chap wouldn't even have noticed."

"But you did," Ben said.

Dawson nodded slowly. "It so happens I'm no ordinary chap. I've done it myself, y'see—picked pockets. I had to. Time was, I was an orphan, a London street boy. It was either steal or starve, and, by Jove, I wasn't going to starve."

Some of the things Dawson had said flashed through Felicity's mind. *My father was head groom for a nobleman . . . he owned a stable in London . . . I was a London street boy . . .*

Now she knew what it was that nagged at her every time she talked to Dawson. He kept giving different versions of his past.

Which one of them was true?

8
A SECRET PAST

Felicity stared at Dawson's bright eyes and his likable face. He seemed so kind and so honest. Yet she had the distinct feeling he was hiding something. If only he would say a little bit more, maybe she could figure it out.

"When was that?" she asked Dawson, trying to get him to talk more about his past. "That you were a street boy?"

"Right before I—" he began but then stopped abruptly. "It's no matter."

He had been about to reveal something, Felicity was sure, and then he'd changed his mind.

What was Dawson hiding ... and why?

Dawson was going on. "The point is, I had to steal to survive. Maybe this girl steals for the same reason. Her guardian is probably forcing her to pick pockets and otherwise rob people of their valuables. Take it from me, all you have to do is bump into a fine-looking gentleman in a crowd, and he'll be so distracted, he'll never notice his timepiece being slipped from a waistcoat pocket."

"Wait a minute!" Felicity said. She'd just thought of her coral necklace. Had Anne stolen it when she'd been jostled into Felicity at the race-track? Felicity told the boys about the incident.

"Oh, yes," said Dawson. "'Tis almost certain she took your necklace. That's how it's done. Befriend a stranger so you can find out what they have to steal. Or bump into someone and then dis-appear before they notice they've been robbed."

Felicity felt like a fool. That's exactly what Anne had done to her! "No wonder she ran from me when I called out to her at the puppet show on the square." She told the boys about seeing Anne fall into the woman with the umbrella. "Anne probably thought I'd discovered that she'd stolen my necklace."

"And she was probably picking the woman's pocket," said Dawson.

"I'll bet her guardian sends her out during Publick Times to steal because there're so many strangers in town," Ben said. "Strangers who won't recognize her—or connect her to him."

"Aye," Dawson said, nodding. "He lets her take all the risks." He clucked. "I figured as much. 'Tis why I didn't have her arrested for trying to steal my money purse. *And* because it was practically empty," he added with a chuckle. Then his tone turned sober. "As for the burrs, Felicity, you shouldn't be angry with the girl for her part in it. I doubt she knew what her guardian planned to do with them."

"I suppose you're right," Felicity said. "It's her guardian I should be angry with, from what you say. He should be arrested for what he did to Penny! But I suppose there's no way to find out who he is."

"Maybe there is," said Ben. "There might be public record of him having been made Anne's guardian, if it happened here in Williamsburg.

Perhaps at Bruton Parish Church or at the courthouse. But you'd need to know *her* last name to
find *him*."

"Which I don't know," said Felicity. Frustration gnawed at her. She felt certain that Anne's
guardian must be responsible for hurting Penny.
Yet there was absolutely nothing she could do
about it.

❧

That night, Dawson slept in the stable. Father
had agreed to hire him and to let him stay with
the Merrimans to take care of Penny. Felicity felt
a little jealous at how easily Penny had accepted
Dawson, but she tried to push it out of her mind.
The important thing was for Penny to get better.

In the morning, Felicity awoke before dawn.
She had lain awake half the night worrying
about Penny and how to find Anne's guardian.
She dressed and waited until the eastern sky
outside her window was faintly pink. Father had
said she wasn't to go outside after dark without

permission. He hadn't said it had to be full day-light. She crept into the hall, tiptoed downstairs, and headed out the back door to the stable.

Dawson was up, and so was Penny. He had already mixed the salve and was spreading it on Penny's back. "How is she?" Felicity asked.

"Pert as a peacock," Dawson replied. "She's been asking for you, though. Kept telling me all night that I wasn't her mistress. I didn't smell quite right."

Pleasure flooded through Felicity. Somehow Dawson had guessed that Felicity might be jealous, and he was trying to make her feel better. He was a mystery to be sure, but did it really matter? Whatever secrets Dawson was keeping were his. She doubted his secrets had anything to do with Penny.

Once Dawson had applied the salve, Felicity fed and watered Penny and Patriot. Any trace of jealousy Felicity felt evaporated when Penny nuzzled her arm as she poured oats into the feed trough. "You're still my pretty lady, aren't you?" Penny whinnied her agreement.

Afterward, Felicity went up to her chamber to wash. If she smelled "horsey," Mrs. Hewitt was bound to make a big fuss.

When Felicity came downstairs, Father and Ben were up, but Mrs. Hewitt hadn't arrived yet. Felicity went to the kitchen house and mixed up a quick batch of sourdough biscuits and sliced and fried some ham. By the time the biscuits came out of the Dutch oven, Mrs. Hewitt still was not there, so Felicity served breakfast to Father, Ben, and Dawson.

There was still no sign of Mrs. Hewitt when they had finished the meal, and Father had become concerned. "I'll make some inquiries," he said as he and the boys were leaving for the store. "I'll let you know, Lissie, what I find out."

After she had cleaned up from breakfast, Felicity began her morning tasks. The sky was overcast and the air held rain, so she couldn't do the washing as she had planned. Instead, she decided, she would tackle the weekly cleaning: dusting and waxing the furniture, sweeping the floors, and polishing the silver.

A SECRET PAST

At first she felt grown-up with Mother's key ring tied to her apron strings, jangling with her every movement. The ring held keys to the kitchen house and the other outbuildings and to all the locked closets and cupboards in the main house. Mother always had the keys close at hand as she worked.

Felicity began dusting in the dining room, but it wasn't long before the heavy keys began to weigh her down. Reaching and stretching to dust the china cabinet with all its shelves, Felicity felt as if she had a millstone at her waist instead of a key ring. She was getting drowsy, too; she'd had so little sleep last night. It was a struggle to keep her eyes open.

She decided that there was no need to carry the keys around, so she dropped them onto the sideboard in the dining room and went back to her dusting. The stillness in the house seemed to ring around her like a bell. With everyone gone, there was no sound except the swish of her feather duster across the furniture. And when she paused for a moment, the silence was as heavy as the thick damask draperies at the window.

Then Felicity heard something upstairs: a *creak-creak,* as if someone was treading very lightly across a wooden floor. Felicity froze.

Was someone in the house?

Felicity stood like a statue, listening. The sound didn't come again. Maybe she had been mistaken, she told herself. Maybe she hadn't heard anything at all.

Or maybe it was the ghost. Lady Margaret's ghost.

Felicity's heart began to pound, and her lungs felt squeezed. She put a hand to her chest. "Stop it," she whispered. "There is no ghost. Lady Margaret has been dead a hundred years."

Felicity forced herself to breathe and to loose the tension from her muscles. She put down her feather duster and made herself walk out into the hallway. All her senses were alert to the slightest sound or movement above her.

Nothing.

She started up the staircase. Lifting each foot was an effort, a struggle against fear. At the top she paused and looked around. There was not a sound or breath of movement. She moved into the upstairs hall, opened every door, and peered inside. Everything was quiet and still, just as it should be.

It was my imagination, she thought, relaxing. *I can't believe I've let Father's ghost story frighten me so.* All the worrying she'd been doing lately must have taken a toll on her nerves, Felicity decided.

Suddenly she realized how exhausted she felt, as if her scare had drained every ounce of energy from her body. The door to her bedchamber stood open, and her four-poster bed with its soft feather mattress looked inviting. *If I lie down for a bit, I'll feel better,* Felicity thought. She went in and got onto the bed. In no time she was asleep.

The next thing she knew, she jerked awake. Through her drowsy fog, an image was fading from her mind. A face? Someone watching her from the doorway? She wasn't sure; it was gone before she could latch onto it.

Lady Margaret . . .

Instantly she was wide-awake. She lay motionless, her heart pounding in fear. After an endless moment, when nothing happened, her heartbeat began to slow. *It was only a dream,* she told herself.

She sat up and rubbed her eyes. Sunlight was streaming through her east-facing window, making dappled shadows on the plastered wall. *Good,* she thought, *it's still morning.* She hadn't slept too long. After she finished her chores, she hoped there'd be time to go to Elizabeth's. She wanted her friend's help in figuring out how to find Anne's guardian. Felicity didn't intend to let him get away with hurting Penny.

She got out of bed and went downstairs. She figured she would finish the dusting and get a start on the bread for dinner. Perhaps she would mix up some dough for cinnamon buns and let it rise while she was gone to Elizabeth's. For that she would need Mother's keys to get sugar and cinnamon from the spice cabinet.

But when she went into the dining room to get the keys off the sideboard, they weren't there!

Felicity panicked. Where had she put those keys? She had to find them. Without the keys, no one could get into the linen closet, the storage closet where the candles were kept, the spice or sugar cabinets, the wine cabinet, the drawer where the good silver was kept, or even the kitchen. The household couldn't function.

If Felicity had lost the keys, Father would be furious! A locksmith would have to be summoned and all the keys remade. And Mother, when she returned, would be terribly disappointed in Felicity.

Frantically, Felicity searched the entire dining room. *No keys.* Without thinking, had she taken the keys upstairs with her? She couldn't have; the keys would have been jangling at her waist, and she'd have remembered that. For that matter, she was certain she didn't have them when she first heard the noise—or thought she'd heard it— while she was dusting, because she remembered noticing the silence when she stopped.

She *had* laid the keys on the sideboard. She knew she had. Why weren't they there?

She pulled a chair out from the table and slumped down in it. "I must be remembering wrong," she said aloud. "If I'd put them on the sideboard, they would still be there."

Keys don't get up and walk away by themselves, she thought. *They must be somewhere in this room, right under my nose.* She wasn't seeing them because she was looking too hard. What she needed was another pair of eyes—Elizabeth!

Felicity jumped up and headed out the door, praying that Elizabeth would be home. She was, and Mrs. Cole was happy to allow Elizabeth to go and help search for the missing keys.

But when they got back to Felicity's house, the keys were on the sideboard, exactly where Felicity thought she had left them.

"Could you have only dreamed the keys were gone?" Elizabeth asked.

"No!" Felicity said. "I distinctly remember looking for them. I was as wide-awake as I am now."

Then an awful thought occurred to her: what if she hadn't imagined the footsteps upstairs? What if it *was* Lady Margaret she had heard? What if Lady Margaret had taken the keys and then returned them? Felicity shivered.

With her words tumbling over one another, Felicity told Elizabeth about Lady Margaret's ghost and about the strange occurrences she'd experienced since the heirlooms had come into Father's possession.

Elizabeth listened, her eyes growing wider as Felicity's story came out. "'Tis almost unbelievable."

"It's true, all of it," Felicity proclaimed. "Though I don't *really* think there's a ghost— at least I don't want to. Yet how else can you explain everything that's happened?"

"I don't know," Elizabeth said, shaking her head. "Maybe if I saw the heirlooms myself..."

"Yes, you must see them!" Felicity exclaimed. She took Elizabeth's hand and led her into the parlor.

Then Felicity's heart leaped into her throat. The heirlooms were gone!

9
STOLEN!

Felicity rushed over to the tilt-top table. In the thin layer of dust on the table, the outline of where the heirlooms had been could clearly be seen. "They were here, Elizabeth," Felicity cried. "They were here!"

"*When* were they here, Felicity? When did you last see the heirlooms?"

Through her panic, Felicity tried to recall. Her thoughts flew backward over the last few days. She'd been so worried about Penny, the heirlooms hadn't been on her mind at all. "The last time I absolutely remember seeing the heirlooms was the night of the race, when I sneaked out to check on Penny and saw the moonlight shining on them."

"We must think," Elizabeth said. "Who's

been in the house since then who might have taken them?"

"Only Mrs. Hewitt," said Felicity. She froze as an idea struck her. "That's why Mrs. Hewitt didn't come today! *She* stole the heirlooms."

Hurriedly Felicity told Elizabeth how Mrs. Hewitt on her first day had stared at Lady Margaret's belongings, how she constantly talked about how poor she was, and how uncomfortable Felicity felt around her.

"Perhaps she'd been waiting for an opportunity to be alone in the house so that she could steal something," Elizabeth suggested.

"You may be right," Felicity agreed. She told Elizabeth how she had forgotten about Mrs. Hewitt in her alarm over Penny. She had hurried to the store to fetch Father and then had gone straight to the stable with Ben and Dawson. "When I came back into the kitchen yesterday, Mrs. Hewitt was already gone. But I thought nothing of it, because she leaves in mid-afternoon.

"It's all my fault," Felicity went on, tears welling in her eyes. "I didn't feel good about

Mrs. Hewitt, but I left her alone here anyway. Ever since Mother went away, I can't seem to do anything right!"

Elizabeth put an arm around Felicity. "You can't blame yourself for this, Felicity. Your first concern was Penny, as it should have been. You couldn't have been expected to know that Mrs. Hewitt was dishonest. The important thing now is getting the heirlooms back. We should go to the store straightaway and tell your father everything."

Felicity swiped her eyes with her sleeve. "You'll come with me?"

"Of course," Elizabeth replied. "What are best friends for?"

The girls started on their way to the store. They'd gone less than half a block when they spotted Father coming toward them. Felicity's first thought was that something was wrong. Why else would Father be coming home in the middle of the morning? Felicity and Elizabeth hurried all the faster to meet him.

Father's face was so grave, Felicity felt

alarmed. "What's happened, Father?" she asked.

Father greeted the girls in a sober voice. "I was coming to the house to tell you what I learned about Mrs. Hewitt. She was taken seriously ill last night—an apoplectic stroke."

Surprise showed on Elizabeth's face. Felicity felt her own jaw drop open. Her mind went blank, and no words would come to her.

"I wanted to tell you myself," Father went on, "rather than sending Ben to do it. I'll do my best to find someone else to help you, though I'm sure I won't have time to do it today. I've never seen the store so busy. 'Tis a good thing we have Dawson to help us."

Felicity still hadn't said anything. Father gave her a concerned look. "Will you be all right, Lissie?"

"Yes, Father," Felicity stammered. "I'm a bit shocked, is all."

"I understand," Father said. "I had quite the same reaction. But Mrs. Hewitt is being tended in her niece's home, and we must trust her recovery to God's will."

"Is Mrs. Hewitt able to receive visitors, Father?" Felicity asked. "The chrysanthemums are in bloom in our garden. I thought I might take her a basket."

Father's eyes brightened. "That would be thoughtful, Lissie. I'll consult her niece and see when you might go by. Now, I must be getting back to the store. Ben and Dawson and I have so much to do there, we won't be coming home for dinner this afternoon. Could you prepare a hearty supper for us tonight without Mrs. Hewitt's help?"

Felicity looked into Father's hopeful face. He had so much on his mind with the store so busy, he shouldn't have to worry about whether Felicity could manage the household alone. "Of course I can," said Felicity, forcing confidence into her voice.

"That's my girl." Father turned to Elizabeth. "Would you ask your mother, Elizabeth, if Felicity could take the midday meal with you? With what has happened, I'd rather she not dine alone."

"I'll ask Mother," Elizabeth replied, "and I'm certain she'll be pleased to have Felicity join us."

Father was off in the other direction before Felicity realized that she had forgotten to tell him about the missing heirlooms. Elizabeth said she had forgotten the heirlooms, too. "The news about Mrs. Hewitt was simply the last thing we expected to hear," said Elizabeth.

Felicity agreed. "Especially since we were certain that the reason she didn't show up today was that she had stolen the heirlooms. Now to find out it was that she was ill . . ."

For a moment they walked in silence, both thinking. Two servant girls passed by, chattering loudly, but Felicity scarcely noticed them. An idea was coming to her that was like a dark cloud blotting out the sun. She hated to voice it to Elizabeth for fear it might be true. At last she said, "If we're considering all possibilities as to who might have taken the heirlooms, I suppose we should consider Dawson." She told Elizabeth about her certainty that Dawson was keeping a secret.

"You're saying you think Dawson is dishonest enough that he might steal from you?"

"No!" Felicity exclaimed. An old man sitting on a bench stared at her, so she walked past him and lowered her voice. "I *don't* think Dawson's dishonest. And I don't really believe he took the heirlooms. At least I don't want to believe he did."

"Then let's think of everyone *else* who might have done it," Elizabeth said. "What about a burglar? Could someone have broken into the house while you were napping and stolen the heirlooms?"

Felicity remembered the eerie feeling she'd had coming home from the race, the feeling that she was being followed. And that same night, she'd had the feeling that someone was hiding in the yard watching her. Could it have been a burglar, watching and waiting for a chance to steal something from the house?

"I don't think so," she said after thinking about it for a moment. "There are lots of other valuables in plain view in the house that *weren't* taken. Mother's silver tea service, for instance, and Sir Edward's dueling pistols. Any ordinary thief would have taken every valuable he could carry. But this thief left them behind."

"What do you mean, any *ordinary* thief?"

"Since only the heirlooms are missing," Felicity said, "whoever took them must have wanted them and nothing else."

The rich smell of spices drifted out of a grocery store up ahead of them. "It does appear that way," said Elizabeth.

"Which means," said Felicity, "there's one possible culprit we haven't mentioned—the one who makes the most sense of all."

Elizabeth stopped walking. A gust whipped her skirt and made it billow out like an umbrella. "Who, Felicity?"

"Lady Margaret's ghost." The grocer's painted sign—three sugar loaves—creaked and swayed above Felicity's head.

For a long time Elizabeth didn't say anything. Felicity could hear the grocer talking to customers inside his store. In the distance, thunder rumbled.

"You think," Elizabeth finally said, "the *ghost* took the heirlooms?"

"Oh, Elizabeth, I just don't know." Frustrated, Felicity started walking again. Her head was beginning to throb. "Part of me doesn't believe in ghosts—the sensible, grown-up part. Yet another part keeps thinking about Lady Margaret all the time."

Elizabeth walked beside Felicity, listening intently.

"From the moment I first heard Father's story," Felicity said, "it seemed as if there was a connection between me and Lady Margaret." She told Elizabeth about the tingling sensation she'd had in her fingers when she first touched the heirlooms.

"That's *frightening*," said Elizabeth.

A man on horseback galloped past in the street, throwing up a swirl of dust. Felicity waited until the dust settled to reply. "I *know*. Yet I can't get it out of my mind. I can't get *her* out of my mind. I keep wondering whether Lady Margaret is distressed that Father plans to sell her belongings to someone outside the family."

"And she's spirited the heirlooms away before your father could sell them?"

"Exactly. I know it doesn't make sense, but I can't get it out of my mind." On the wind came another grumble of thunder. Felicity glanced up. Dark-tinged clouds rolled fast across the sky.

"But ghosts don't exist, Felicity."

"How do we know?" asked Felicity. "Sir Edward believed in his wife's ghost enough that he left England and sailed to the colonies, trying to escape her. And still she followed him." She paused. "It sounds crazy, but I've been feeling a sort of presence around me ever since the heirlooms arrived."

"Are you certain you haven't imagined it?"

"No, I'm *not* certain. But I have felt *something*, as surely as I feel the wind blowing now."

"A very cold wind," Elizabeth said, shivering. Spatters of rain were gusting down on the brisk breeze. "Oh, Felicity, let's not talk about Lady Margaret anymore. It makes my flesh creep."

"We won't, then," Felicity said, "for now, anyway. But let's not rule her out, either."

Elizabeth nodded. "Come, let's hurry to my house. It's starting to rain."

10

MORE DISAPPEARANCES

The girls made it to Elizabeth's house right
before the sky opened up and rain poured down.
While they were eating with Mrs. Cole and
Elizabeth's sister, Annabelle, it began to storm
so violently that thunder shook the whole
house and made the windows rattle. Mrs. Cole
wouldn't allow Felicity to go home until the
worst of the storm had blown over.

When Felicity finally did leave, it was mid-
afternoon. Mrs. Cole had insisted that Felicity
borrow one of Annabelle's old capes for the walk
home. The rain was only a drizzle, yet the air
felt much colder. Felicity pulled the cape closer
around her shoulders. The miserable weather still
seemed to sink into her bones, and it made her
feel miserable, too.

She started thinking of Mother's return in little more than a week. With all that had happened, Felicity hadn't done very well at living up to Mother's expectations. When Felicity was at her own front gate, she remembered that Father had asked her to fix a hearty meal for supper. It occurred to her that she'd never gotten around to mixing up the cinnamon buns she'd planned this morning.

How could I have gone all day without thinking about tonight's meal?

Once again she had neglected her responsibilities. Now she had let Father down as well as Mother.

Felicity's mood dipped lower. Perhaps Mother had been wrong to put her confidence in Felicity. Felicity didn't feel at all like the grown-up young gentlewoman Mother thought she was—at least not now, when everything Felicity did seemed to go wrong.

Then Felicity squared her shoulders. Mother always said there was no use crying over spilt milk, which meant there was no use wasting time feeling bad about something in the past. Mother wouldn't return for some days yet. Felicity determined she would do better and make Mother—and Father—proud of her.

Felicity tried to think of a hearty meal for Father that could be prepared quickly. It came to her like magic: boiled potatoes and turnips with bread and cheese to go along, and perhaps leftover apple tarts for dessert. She would need potatoes and turnips from the cellar. Everything else for the meal was in the pie safe in the kitchen.

Without going inside, Felicity went around to the back of the house. The cellar steps were beside the back door. Her head bowed against the drizzle, she reached down to pull up the cellar doors and saw something lying on the ground at the base of the back steps. She stooped to pick it up.

Her coral necklace!

The necklace must have been here all along. With both Mother and Rose gone, the back door was seldom used. But Felicity had gone in and out this way several times the evening of the race to check on Penny in the stable. The necklace must have slipped off without Felicity noticing.

So Anne hadn't stolen her necklace after all. Felicity had jumped to the wrong conclusion about Anne because Dawson had said she'd tried to steal from *him.*

Had she also jumped to a wrong conclusion about Anne's guardian? After all, Felicity had no proof that the burrs Anne collected for him were used to harm Penny. Somehow, Felicity needed to find Anne and talk to her. Maybe Anne could tell her what her guardian had done with the burrs.

Then Felicity remembered Ben's comment that there might be a public record of someone being made Anne's guardian, and it gave her an idea. She would go to Bruton Parish Church and talk to the minister. The Reverend Mr. Ullfers knew everyone in the parish. He might be able to help Felicity locate Anne or learn who her guardian was.

For now, though, Felicity had a meal to

prepare. Slipping the coral necklace into her pocket, she retrieved potatoes and turnips from the cellar. Then she went inside, got Mother's keys, and unlocked the kitchen house. With wood from the wood box, she rekindled the kitchen fire. While she was waiting for the fire to get hot, she peeled the vegetables and went to the pie safe to get out the bread and cheese and tarts.

But the pie safe was empty!

Felicity stared. She knew the bread had been here last night. She had cut some slices herself to serve for supper. A wheel of hard yellow cheese had been here at suppertime, too, and four apple tarts that Mrs. Hewitt had baked before she left yesterday.

All gone. Who had taken them?

Felicity's thoughts skittered among possibilities. Obviously it couldn't have been Mrs. Hewitt, since Felicity had seen the food at suppertime last night *after* Mrs. Hewitt left. Was it Dawson, perhaps? But Dawson had no need to steal food, since he was taking his meals with the Merrimans.

LADY MARGARET'S GHOST

Had an intruder come in while Felicity was at Elizabeth's and taken only what he needed to survive? The kitchen house was kept locked, though, and the key was on Mother's key ring.

Felicity's heart thudded as she remembered the key ring being missing this morning. Maybe someone had come in while she was napping, stolen the food and Lady Margaret's silver, returned the keys, and made off with the loot. What thief in his right mind, though, would *return* keys? It didn't make sense.

Then a shudder went down her spine. Could Lady Margaret be responsible? Did a ghost eat?

"Don't be ridiculous," Felicity said aloud. "Of course ghosts don't eat. There *is* no such thing as ghosts."

The same person—and it *was* a person, Felicity assured herself—who took the keys must have taken the food, even if it *didn't* make sense that the keys had been returned.

She decided to check the other cupboards and closets in the house to see if anything else was missing. She tried to ignore the uncomfortable

idea that the thief might still be lurking somewhere nearby. The odds of that were small, she
told herself. Whoever had stolen the food and
the silver was probably long gone.

Yet her pulse beat faster as she banked the
fire and hurried from the kitchen, locking the
door behind her. It was still drizzling, but Felicity
barely noticed as she hurried back into the
house. Her footsteps rang on the wooden floor
of the hall. In the dining room, she unlocked first
the wine cabinet and then the sugar and spice
cabinets. Nothing seemed amiss.

Taking a long, deliberate breath, Felicity went
upstairs. She was sweating, although the house
was cold. The large storage cupboard was at the
far end of the upstairs hall. Felicity wiped her
clammy palms on her skirt and fumbled with
the keys. Finding the right one, she slipped it
into the keyhole. It turned with a *click.* The bed
linens, coverlets, and blankets were folded neatly
on the upper shelves. A ceramic jar of home-
made scented soaps and the large brass candle
box took up the bottom shelf.

Lady Margaret's Ghost

Felicity scanned the shelves; then her hand flew up to the coverlets. Mother's best chariot-wheel-pattern coverlet should have been on top, but it wasn't. Maybe it had been put back in the wrong place. She flipped through all the linens and the other coverlets and blankets. The chariot-wheel coverlet wasn't there.

At a glance Felicity could tell that no soap was missing from the jar. She opened the brass candle box. Half of the candles were gone. She knew Mother had filled the box with newly made candles before she'd left on her trip.

Felicity swallowed. What did it mean? Why would a thief steal such random items?

Suddenly, fragments from Father's story sprang into her mind, dark and frightening: *Lady Margaret's ghost, gliding down the stairs with a lighted candle . . . at the linen closet, fetching a blanket to cover her dead child . . .*

"No," Felicity whispered. Then, more loudly, she repeated, "No, I don't believe it!" She slammed the cupboard door shut and locked it. There was another explanation for all the things that were going missing—one that didn't involve a ghost. Felicity simply had to figure out what it was.

Turning the question over in her mind, she went downstairs. Maybe if she combed through the parlor, she could find a clue that would help her figure out who had taken the heirlooms and the other missing items. She went through the hallway and to the parlor doors.

There she stopped, shock clenching her insides. On the tilt-top table, as if it had never been gone, sat Lady Margaret's silver!

11
DAWSON'S THEFT

A chill struck Felicity deep in the pit of her
stomach. She must be seeing things, or dreaming.
Yet she knew she was awake.

She rushed to the table and touched the heirlooms. The silver was cold and hard—and real.
She certainly hadn't dreamed the heirlooms
being gone. Elizabeth had been beside her when
they discovered the silver was gone.

Fear thumped through Felicity. All she
wanted to do was get out of the house. She shot
a glance out the parlor window. The storm had
picked up again. Rain hammered against the
windowpanes and whipped through the apple
tree outside. Felicity didn't care. She snatched
a cloak from a hook in the hall and bolted out
the door.

DAWSON'S THEFT

Across the street, she glimpsed a man standing in the downpour, staring at the house. *Probably lost.* For a fleeting moment she wondered if she should stop and ask him if he needed help finding someone's house. Any other time she would have helped him, but now her only thought was getting to Elizabeth's.

Pulling the cloak's hood low to shield her face from the rain, Felicity ran all the way to her friend's house. By the time she got there, she was soaked and shivering. Mrs. Cole clucked over her and insisted she change into dry clothes of Elizabeth's.

Elizabeth took Felicity up to her bedchamber. The afternoon was so dark and chilly that candles had been lit, and a fire crackled in the grate. While Felicity peeled off her wet things and put on the dry ones Elizabeth gave her, the girls talked. Felicity told Elizabeth everything that had happened.

Felicity sank onto Elizabeth's bed. "I don't know what to think. I'm beginning to believe there really *is* a ghost. And for some reason, the only person Lady Margaret is interested in is me!" A sob came up into her throat, and Felicity swallowed fiercely to suppress it.

"There now," Elizabeth said, sitting down beside her and putting an arm around her. "We should try to figure out whether there's some other explanation before we jump to conclusions about a ghost."

"What other explanation could there possibly be," Felicity protested, "for things disappearing and reappearing again?"

"I don't know," Elizabeth said, "but thinking of a ghost haunting your house frightens the wits out of me. I'd much rather try to talk ourselves out of the possibility. Wouldn't you?"

Quietly Felicity nodded. For a moment there was no sound but the snapping of the flames and the rain drumming on the windows.

"Let's think," said Elizabeth. "We'll have to rule out Mrs. Hewitt entirely. She could have taken the silver before she got sick, but, as ill as she is, she couldn't possibly have returned it. And it couldn't have been a burglar breaking into the house; a burglar would never have returned the silver."

Elizabeth paused as if she was thinking. The candle on the nightstand cast a fluttering glow on her face. "Lissie," she finally said, with reluctance in her voice. "Do you think it *could* have been Dawson? Could he have taken everything, and then had an attack of conscience and returned the heirlooms?"

The same thought had been on Felicity's mind, heavy as lead. She felt relieved that Elizabeth had brought it up first. "I just don't want to believe he would steal from us," she said.

Elizabeth put a hand on Felicity's knee. "I know you're fond of Dawson. But what do you really know about him? You said he had a secret. What made you think so?"

Felicity explained how Dawson seemed to sidestep questions about his past and how the things that he did say seemed to contradict one another. "Once he said his father was head groom in a nobleman's stable, and later he said that his father owned a stable in London. How could it be both? And another time he admitted to being a street boy who picked people's pockets."

"You're thinking that if he stole once, he might do it again," Elizabeth said. Downstairs, someone slammed a door.

Felicity stared miserably into the fire. Much as she hated to admit it, it *was* what she had been thinking. "He did say picking pockets was the only way he could survive."

"I suppose when they're desperate, people will do things they wouldn't ordinarily do," Elizabeth said.

Felicity jumped up and strode to the fireplace. She turned to Elizabeth. "I keep wondering just how desperate he is, Elizabeth. When we met him, he said he was nearly penniless, remember?"

Elizabeth said she did.

"And now he may be wondering what he's going to do once Publick Times are over next week, when Father won't need him at the store any longer," Felicity went on. "By then, Penny's sores will be healing. Dawson must be thinking that Father will expect him to move out of the stable soon. He won't have a place to live or food to eat—"

Then Felicity gasped. "Oh, Elizabeth! I just thought of something."

In a rush of words, she told Elizabeth how oddly Dawson had acted yesterday on the way home from the store. "He suddenly bolted across the street and nearly ran all the way to my house, as if he was trying to get *away* from somebody. What if he's a runaway, Elizabeth—an indentured servant or an apprentice running away from his master?"

Elizabeth wrinkled her forehead in a thoughtful manner. "He'd be desperate, then, to find a place to sleep off the street. Less chance of him being discovered by whoever's looking for him."

"And the things missing from our house make more sense," Felicity said.

"A blanket, candles, food," said Elizabeth, counting off the items on her fingers. "All provisions needed for a long trip." She raised an eyebrow. "An escape from Williamsburg, perhaps?"

"Yes," Felicity said. "He'd need money for a trip like that, as well as provisions. Maybe he stole the silver, planning to sell it, but he felt so guilty, he returned it." Even talking about the possibility that Dawson might have taken the heirlooms made her feel sick. How she wished there was someone else to blame for the theft!

"He would have waited till the last minute to take what he needed, I would think," said Elizabeth. "So he must be planning to flee soon. Maybe even tonight."

Felicity nodded. "He's got to know it won't be long until we discover things are missing." She paced to the middle of the room and held out her arms in a gesture of frustration. "If only he had asked Father for help, Elizabeth, instead of stealing from us!"

Elizabeth got up, went to Felicity, and clutched her hands. "Maybe if we go to the store now and talk to Dawson, he'll admit everything and he *will* ask your father for help."

Felicity gave Elizabeth's hands a squeeze.

"That's a wonderful idea. But let's hurry! I still have supper to make for Father."

"We'll go this minute," Elizabeth said. "Mother asked me to get some things at the store for her anyway. When we get back, you can change into your own clothes and be on your way."

❦

The rain had stopped, and the pale sunlight of late afternoon glistened on the wet grass and in the puddles on the street as the girls walked to the store. Two women were coming out of the store as Felicity and Elizabeth went in. The women held the door open for Felicity, and she let it close behind her with a soft thud.

She scanned the store—the shelves from floor to ceiling, baskets hanging from the rafters, barrels and boxes of wares everywhere. She didn't see Father or Ben, but she spotted Dawson crouched beside a shelf in back. She motioned to Elizabeth to follow her and started toward him.

Just then, the wooden floor creaked. Dawson lifted his head, and Felicity glimpsed something that made her heart sink. In Dawson's hand was one of the store's best pocketknives, and he had been about to slip it inside his waistcoat!

12
A DARING PLAN

"Felicity! And Elizabeth!" Dawson stood up, his usual friendly grin spreading across his face. "You startled me!" He had turned his hand over so that the knife was hidden inside his fingers.

"That's obvious," Felicity said. Blood pounded in her temples. "Since you were about to steal from my father."

Dawson's cheeks flamed. "What do you mean?"

"The pocketknife," Felicity said coldly. "You were getting ready to steal it."

"We saw you," Elizabeth added.

"I'm not a thief!" Dawson's eyes flashed angrily.

"Then how do you explain the things you took from our house?" Felicity countered. "The food and the candles and the blanket? And Lady Margaret's silver?"

"If you were a runaway," Elizabeth threw in, "all you had to do was talk to Mr. Merriman—"

"I don't have to listen to this," Dawson interrupted bitterly. His voice rose to a louder pitch. "Take your precious pocketknife, Miss Merriman, and give it to your father when he returns." He shoved the knife into Felicity's hand. "I'm on my way out, and you'll not see me again, I promise you."

Suddenly the storeroom door was flung open, and Ben rushed out. "What's going on? I could hear the yelling all the way back in the storeroom."

Dawson jutted out his chin. "Felicity thinks I've been stealing from her father."

Ben drew down his brows. "Why would you think that, Lissie?"

"Because of this," Felicity said, holding up the knife. "We caught him trying to take it."

"And rightly so!" Ben exclaimed. "Your father promised a knife to Dawson as part of his wages.

Mr. Merriman had to go out to conduct some business, and he told Dawson to pick out any knife he wanted while he was gone."

Ben's words dashed Felicity's anger like a bucketful of water thrown on a fire. Slowly, miserably, it dawned on her how badly she had misjudged Dawson. She knew she owed Dawson an apology, but she was too ashamed of herself to say it.

Elizabeth spoke instead. "We're so sorry, Dawson. We should have trusted you."

"Yes," Felicity managed. "We were wrong."

"Why would you make such an accusation?" Ben asked. Dawson's fierce stare seemed to ask the same question.

Felicity fumbled for words. "It's just . . . well . . . some things were missing from the house, and then we saw Dawson taking the knife . . ."

"So you naturally assumed I was *stealing* it," Dawson spit out.

"We thought you might be desperate for money," Elizabeth said. She and Felicity explained how they'd thought Dawson was keeping secrets about his past and that he might be running away from a cruel master.

When they'd finished, Ben and Dawson exchanged a knowing glance. "They weren't so far from the truth after all," Ben said.

"I suppose they weren't," Dawson said. His voice was strained but not as angry.

Apparently Ben was in on Dawson's secret—whatever it was. "What *is* the truth?" Felicity demanded.

"Dawson *has* been hiding from someone," Ben said, "but your father knows all about it."

"Everything I told you about my past is true," Dawson said. "I'm *not* a liar." He crossed his arms defensively. "My father *was* in charge of Lord Hathaway's stables, in York, England, near where you're from, Elizabeth."

"I knew I recognized your accent," Elizabeth said.

He nodded and went on. "When Lord Hathaway died, he left my father some money, enough to buy a stable in London. That went well for a few years, until Father passed away

and the stable was sold to pay his debts. I was left
to fend for myself on the streets, picking pockets
to survive.

"Late one night, outside a tavern near the
docks, my luck ran out. The sailors I tried to steal
from weren't as drunk as I thought. They beat
me senseless and kidnapped me to work on their
ship. The next day I woke up and found myself
at sea, aboard a ship bound for America. I was
forced to work as a cabin boy. I would have liked
life at sea, but the ship's captain was as cruel
a man as you'll ever meet, and his first mate
wasn't much better. As soon as we docked here
in Virginia, I jumped ship."

Suddenly Felicity understood. "So it was
someone from the ship that you saw the other
day?"

"The captain's mate was one of the sailors
we saw arguing. I guess he was sent to look for
me. I knew eventually the ship would leave port
with him aboard, and I'd be safe. I only had to
bide my time and keep out of sight. So I asked
your father if I could stay and work for him for

a while. He said he needed extra help during Publick Times and he'd be happy to do what he could for me."

Felicity felt wretched. "Dawson, I hope you'll forgive us for what we said."

Hurt still showed on Dawson's face, but he shrugged. "It was a mistake. Think nothing of it." At that moment the bell over the front door jingled. Customers were coming into the store: a man and a woman with three small children.

"Could you see to them, Dawson?" Ben asked. Dawson headed to the front counter, and Ben, in a low voice, said to Felicity, "What's this about things missing from the house?"

"Nothing," Felicity said quickly. "Probably just something I've overlooked." She was too embarrassed to admit that she was afraid of Lady Margaret's ghost. All she wanted to do was escape Ben's questions. "Well, Ben, Elizabeth and I should be going."

Ben looked perplexed. "Why did you come in the first place?"

"It . . . wasn't important." Before Ben could say

anything else, Felicity took Elizabeth's arm and pulled her toward the door. Once they were outside, Felicity sank back against the store's white clapboard wall and closed her eyes. "That was a disaster."

"And you didn't even let me do Mother's shopping," Elizabeth said, sounding annoyed.

"We'll go to the grocer's," Felicity promised. "I'm sorry. I was too embarrassed to stay any longer."

"We did make a terrible mistake about Dawson," Elizabeth admitted.

They were silent for a moment. Felicity's gaze fixed on a horse tied to a hitching post across the street. She said, "You realize what this means, don't you, Elizabeth? If Dawson isn't the thief . . ."

Elizabeth leaned back against the wall, too. "The only culprit we have left is Lady Margaret."

Felicity didn't reply. The thought was too discouraging—and frightening. She watched a man come out of a shop, untie the horse, mount, and ride away. Absently her hand went into her pocket and her fingers closed around the cool, round beads of the coral necklace.

Anne. In all the uproar over Dawson, Felicity had forgotten that she'd meant to talk to the minister about how to find Anne's guardian.

An idea leaped into her mind, a way to kill two birds with one stone. If anyone knew how to get rid of a ghost, it should be the Reverend Mr. Ullfers. And perhaps he could tell them something about Anne and her guardian as well. Felicity explained her plan to Elizabeth.

Elizabeth agreed to the plan. "The church isn't far from my house. We can do Mother's shopping after we talk to the minister."

Felicity and Elizabeth hurried to Bruton Parish Church. Orange and gold tinged the leaves of the huge spreading trees in the church-yard. Inside the church, they found the Reverend Mr. Ullfers sitting in one of the white, high-backed pews, reading the Bible. He was dressed in a long black robe with a white cravat at his throat. At the sound of the great wooden doors closing behind the girls, he looked up.

A Daring Plan

"Oh, we're disturbing you," Felicity said. Her voice echoed in the stillness of the empty sanctuary, and she was awed and a little afraid.

But the friendly tone of the minister's voice put her at ease. "Not at all. Come, come." He beckoned for the girls to enter the square, box-like pew where he sat. When they had come through the small pew door and seated themselves across from him, he said, "Tell me what I can do for you."

"What do you know about ghosts?" Felicity ventured.

The minister smiled. "You're not talking about the blessed Trinity, I presume—Father, Son, and Holy Ghost?"

"No," Elizabeth said. "Ordinary ghosts. Are they real?"

The minister laced his fingers together so that the wide sleeves of his robe hid his hands. "You want to know whether our spirits are capable of roaming the earth after the death of the physical body . . . as apparitions. Ghosts, if you will."

"Yes," Felicity and Elizabeth said together.

Felicity hoped he didn't think the question was childish.

"Ahh, a delicate question." The minister drew out his hand and scratched his head. "Some very devout people believe in the existence of ghosts, and others, equally devout, insist that ghosts are so much superstitious nonsense."

"What do you believe, sir?" Felicity asked.

He looked thoughtful. "Let's just say that I'm open-minded in the matter."

"You don't think it's nonsense, then, to believe in ghosts?" Elizabeth asked.

"Certainly not," he replied. "There are people in this parish who confess to having been visited by otherworldly beings. Ghosts, they would tell you, are restless spirits disturbed about something that happened to them in life or worried about the people they cared about."

Suddenly Felicity remembered what Father had said about Lady Margaret: that she was distressed because her husband had no child to carry on the Merriman name. It gave her an idea. "Suppose that was true, sir," Felicity said, "and the ghost could be reassured that what she was worried about *didn't* happen after all. Do you think the ghost would stop its roaming and be at peace?"

"It seems a reasonable theory to me," he said.

A weight seemed to lift from Felicity's shoulders. If she could do something about Lady Margaret, Felicity wouldn't feel so hopeless or so frightened. Felicity glanced at Elizabeth. Elizabeth smiled reassuringly. She must feel the same way.

"I hope I've helped," the minister said.

"You have," Felicity replied.

"We have another question for you," Elizabeth added. "If you don't mind." She looked at Felicity. Felicity had been trying to figure out how to phrase the question about Anne's guardian without giving away too much information.

"We've been trying to find someone," Felicity plunged in. "The guardian of a girl we met at the fair a few days ago. The girl's name is Anne."

"She's about our age," Elizabeth added, "and

she has curly red hair and a face full of freckles."

The minister wrinkled his forehead as if he was thinking. "I do know of a girl in the parish who fits that description. The gentleman who is her guardian was a friend of the girl's father. When her parents died, there were no relatives, and this man and his wife agreed to take her in. Otherwise the girl would have gone to the almshouse. The gentleman's name is William Yancey."

Felicity's heart began to pound. *William Yancey.* Could it be the same fine gentleman who had made a bet on Penny at the race? It had to be. A startled look shot between Felicity and Elizabeth.

"Mr. Yancey and his wife live on Nicholson Street, near the jail," the Reverend Mr. Ullfers went on. "I'd be happy to give him a message for you, if you like."

"Er, no," Felicity stammered. "Thank you just the same." She stood up, eager to get away before the minister could question them about why they wanted to find Mr. Yancey.

Elizabeth stood up, too. "We're obliged, sir. Thank you for your time."

He nodded graciously. "I'm glad I could be of assistance."

Felicity and Elizabeth were both breathless from excitement as they hurried from the church. Outside, they stood in the long shadow of the churchyard wall and talked. "It's him, Elizabeth," Felicity said. "Mr. Yancey. He's the one who tried to hurt Penny!"

"It makes perfect sense," Elizabeth said. "Remember? He said that he and Mr. Minton had placed large bets on their horses in the race. When he saw Penny, he must have thought she threatened his chances of winning all that money. As soon as he left us, he must have found Anne and ordered her to gather the burrs."

"He probably didn't place a bet on Penny at all," Felicity said. "He probably only pretended he did so that he could come back to talk to me and get near Penny again."

"There was so much confusion with all the people around us before the race," Elizabeth said. "Mr. Yancey could have hidden the burrs in his coat and slipped them under Penny's saddle blanket while we were distracted."

"I'm sure that's exactly what happened," Felicity said, anger building inside her. She clenched her fists. "Wait until I tell Father what that scoundrel did to Penny!"

"Your father can have Mr. Yancey arrested for hurting Penny," Elizabeth said, "and for cheating the people who placed bets on her in the race."

"I'll talk to Father tonight as soon as he gets home," Felicity said. The helplessness and frustration she'd felt for so many days gave way to a sense of satisfaction. "And you know what else, Elizabeth? I've figured out what I'm going to do about Lady Margaret."

Felicity described her daring plan: Tonight, after Father was asleep, Felicity was going to go *looking* for Lady Margaret. She told Elizabeth how Lady Margaret had wanted her husband to have a son to carry on his name.

"Instead of running away from the ghost," Felicity said, "I'll talk to her and tell her that

Edward remarried and had children and grandchildren, and that the Merriman family is still thriving a hundred years later. But I'll tell her that Edward never forgot her, and that the story of her love for him was passed down to every generation."

"That ought to make any ghost happy," said Elizabeth. "But how do you plan to find her, Lissie?"

"Tonight, after everyone is asleep, I'll go to the parlor, sit by the heirlooms, and wait for her," said Felicity.

"And this time," she added with resolve, "*nothing* will scare me away. If there *is* a ghost in our house, Elizabeth, I'm going to find her."

13
SEARCH FOR A GHOST

Felicity didn't get a chance to talk to Father that night about Mr. Yancey. Father had hurt his back at the store lifting some heavy barrels, and Dr. Galt, the apothecary, had given him a powder to take for pain and had told him to go to bed as soon as he got home.

"Dr. Galt assured me my back would be much better in the morning after a good night's rest," Father told Felicity. He apologized for not being able to eat the supper he had asked Felicity to make. "My back is so painful, I don't have much of an appetite," he explained.

"That's all right, Father," Felicity said. "I'm sure Ben and Dawson will be glad to eat your portion." In truth, she was relieved. When Felicity had finally gotten home that afternoon, it had been too late to cook potatoes and turnips. She'd had to quickly stew some dried apples and mix up and bake a batch of cornbread, which wasn't exactly the hearty meal Father had been looking forward to.

Felicity figured that tomorrow would be soon enough to tell Father about Mr. Yancey. She was anxious anyway about her plan to go looking for Lady Margaret. Felicity was worried she might lose her courage when she came face-to-face with the ghost, just as she had so many times before.

As Felicity lay in bed waiting until Father and Ben were asleep, she tried to think over what she would say to Lady Margaret. But she was so exhausted from the day's events that before she knew it, she had dozed off.

She was awakened by the clock downstairs striking twelve. Then she froze, her skin prickling in terror. Through the crack under her door she'd glimpsed a faint, flickering light—there and then gone—as if someone with a candle had passed by her bedchamber.

Who could it be but Lady Margaret?

A wave of panic rose in Felicity's throat, but she forced it down. She knew she had to face the ghost—or whatever was out there. If she didn't, the fear she'd lived with these last few days would go on and on.

Gathering her courage, Felicity slid out of bed and slipped on a dressing gown over her night shift. She went to her chamber door, opened it, and peered out. She scanned the dark hall, then crept out to the stairway landing and looked down to the front hall. A light was just disappearing into the parlor. Then the parlor double doors softly thudded shut.

Felicity forced herself to move down the stairs, one by one, in the darkness. On silent cat's feet she padded across the hall and grasped the parlor's brass doorknobs with her icy hands. For a moment she hesitated; then she flung the doors open.

From the darkness, images jumped out at her: moonlight through the broken shutter, and a figure—not a ghost, but flesh and blood. Felicity saw the stark white of an oversized mob cap and a halo of candlelight on a dirty freckled face.

It was Anne! In one hand Anne held a candle and in the other a bundle—a bundle that was wrapped in Mother's chariot-wheel coverlet.

"*You're* the thief?" Felicity was struggling to understand how Anne could be standing in her parlor in the middle of the night.

"Please, miss," Anne begged. "I meant no harm. I'm leaving now. I swear, I am."

Felicity's thoughts were whirling: *How did Anne know where I live? How did she get into the house? Was she planning to steal the heirlooms tonight? And why does she have Mother's coverlet*?

Then, with a sick feeling, Felicity realized what must have happened. At the race, she had told Anne about Lady Margaret's heirlooms. Anne must have planned to steal them all along. Perhaps she had taken whatever else struck her fancy, too—like Mother's coverlet. Hurt and angry, Felicity blurted out her suspicions to Anne.

"No," Anne said. "That's not what happened. Let me explain." The flickering candle she held illuminated the angles of her thin, pinched face. Tears glistened on her cheeks, and she was trembling.

Felicity felt sorry for her. "You should sit down," Felicity told her. "Here, give me the candle."

Anne blinked and then handed the candle to Felicity. Like a rag doll, she collapsed onto the sofa and let the bundle drop beside her. Felicity set the candle in an empty candlestick on the end table beside the sofa. Then she leaned against the deep windowsill next to the fireplace, directly across from Anne. "Now you can explain," she said gently but firmly.

Anne seemed to have trouble getting started. She looked down into her lap and fiddled with the folds of her skirt. "I didn't come into the parlor tonight to *steal* the silver, y'see. I only wanted another glimpse of it. I've never seen anything so lovely." Her voice had taken on an element of wonder. "The way the silver on the brush and comb gleams, you can see your face in it. Just like a looking glass."

"*Anne*." Impatience brimmed inside Felicity. "*Please.* We're not talking about looking glasses. We're talking about valuable family heirlooms, which you were trying to steal." Then it dawned on her what Anne had said. "*Another* glimpse of the silver? What did you mean by that?"

Anne leaned forward, the glow of yellow candlelight on her face. "I took 'em yesterday, y'see. Your heirlooms. But that was before I knew how much they meant to you. Then when I heard you and your friend talking about 'em—I was hiding in the closet, y'see—I felt so bad, I went and put 'em back as soon as you had gone—"

"Wait a minute!" Felicity said, feeling bewildered by everything Anne was saying. "You took the heirlooms *yesterday?* How long have you been in the house?"

Without waiting for an answer, she added, "It was *you* who took Mother's keys, too, wasn't it? And the food and candles. And of course Mother's coverlet." Felicity jutted her chin toward the bundle. "But how—I don't understand any of this. How did you get inside?

When? And why did you do it?"

"I should start at the beginning—"

"The beginning," Felicity interrupted, "was at the racetrack. When you collected sweet gum burrs for your guardian to use to hurt my horse so that she couldn't run her best in the race."

"To hurt your horse?"

In the fluttering glow of the candle, Felicity saw total surprise and confusion on Anne's face. She remembered Dawson's guess that Anne had been blindly obeying her guardian's order. "You didn't know what your guardian wanted the burrs for, did you?"

Anne shook her head vigorously. "I don't dare question him—ever." Then she added softly, "Unless I want a beating."

Felicity had nearly forgotten Dawson's suspicion that Anne's guardian was mistreating her. She felt sympathy stirring, though she didn't want to give in to it. Not until she'd had the truth from Anne—about everything. "Your guardian is William Yancey, isn't he?"

Anne nodded.

"He beats you?"

"All the time," Anne said. "So does his wife. And they threaten to leave me in the poorhouse if I don't do what they say. Yet they make me call them Father and Mother Yancey, as if they cared for me. All they really care about, though, is the work I do for them—and what they make me steal for them."

Dawson was right again, Felicity thought. But she let Anne go on.

"Whenever there's a public event in town, they make me go out into the crowd, steal from people, and bring back whatever I've stolen. If what I bring isn't enough, I can expect a beating. That's what happened the day of the race. I hadn't been able to steal anything but your necklace." She stared down at the floor, avoiding Felicity's gaze.

"So you *did* take it," Felicity said. "But... why did I find it on the back steps?"

"I put it there," Anne said.

Felicity stood up. She took a few steps toward Anne and held her arms out in a gesture of confusion. "You stole the heirlooms and put them back. You stole my necklace and put *it* back. That doesn't make sense, Anne."

"It does," Anne said, "if you'll let me finish."

Felicity pushed her impatience aside and seated herself in the wing chair nearest Anne. "Go on."

Anne squeezed her eyes shut, as if to stop tears. After a moment, she opened them and continued. "The day of the race, Father Yancey was furious because all I'd been able to steal was your necklace. He told me it was a cheap trinket and threw it back at me."

"That necklace is not cheap!" Felicity said. "It was my mother's—"

"*I* loved the necklace," Anne broke in. "'Twas why I kept it. But listen, if you will." Anne's tone was so insistent, Felicity fell silent, determined not to interrupt again.

Anne's hand went to the bundle beside her, and she absently stroked the fringed edge of the coverlet. "Father Yancey boxed my ears and threatened me with a thrashing if I couldn't do better. He was in a foul mood because his horse had lost, and I was terrible scared.

"Before I knew it, I'd blurted out what you told me about the redheaded lady's silver and how you were alone during the day. He made me tell him your name, and he smiled an awful smile and said he knew of your father and his prosperous store."

The image of that awful smile made Felicity shiver. The candle sputtered, and Anne went on. "He told me I had to find you again and follow you home and, somehow, get in your house and steal the silver pieces. He said if I didn't bring the silver back to him, he'd make me wish I'd never been born."

Felicity was horror-struck. "He *said* that?"

"Oh, *yes*. And he meant it, too." With her sleeve, Anne swiped at tears Felicity couldn't see. "I didn't know how I was going to find you in all that crowd of people, but I got lucky and you found *me*."

Felicity leaned toward Anne, her elbows braced on her knees. "Was that when I saw you at the puppet show booth and you ran away?"

Anne nodded. "I hid in the crowd and followed you when you started home."

"I thought there was someone following me that day!" Excited, Felicity sat up straight. "And it was you I saw in the yard that night."

"Yes," Anne said quietly. "I was *afraid* you'd seen me, and I didn't know what I was going to do if you discovered me. But all of a sudden, you dashed for the house, like you'd seen a ghost or something."

It was too close to the truth, and Felicity felt herself blush. She hoped it was too dark in the parlor for Anne to notice. Suddenly she realized how Anne had gotten into the house. "You discovered I'd left the door unlatched, didn't you?"

Anne shrugged. "You ran in so fast, I thought you might have. It made it easier that I didn't have to break a window to get in."

She told Felicity how she'd hidden in the attic that night and all the next day, waiting for an opportunity to steal the heirlooms. Every time she'd ventured out, she said, she'd heard voices or had seen somebody in the house.

"I dreaded another night in that attic," Anne went on, "but I didn't have a choice. I couldn't go back to Father Yancey empty-handed. The *next* morning, though, when I sneaked out from the attic, everything was quiet, so I came in here and took the silver pieces. I figured that perhaps you'd gone out to the market."

"I was here," Felicity said miserably, "but I was asleep." Her cheeks burned. How she hated to admit she'd been napping in the middle of the morning.

"I found that out," Anne said. "When I passed your bedchamber, I saw you in bed, and it frightened the wits out of me."

"Then I *did* see someone looking at me when I woke up! I thought it was a dream."

"I hid until I heard the front door slam," Anne said. "I knew then that you really had gone out."

"You must have taken Mother's keys, too," Felicity said. "What'd you have in mind? Stealing everything we had under lock and key?"

"Not everything." Anne's voice was dull.

"Only enough to make Father Yancey happy. I knew he'd be angry that it had taken me so long to get him the silver."

Felicity's conscience twitched. She shouldn't have lost her temper with Anne. She bit her lip and tried harder to listen.

"But then I had the idea," Anne went on, "that I could sell the heirlooms myself and make enough money to get away from the Yanceys forever. I'm good at sewing—good enough, I thought, to work as a seamstress somewhere far from Williamsburg." Her plan, she told Felicity, was to hide in the attic until the hours before dawn, and then make her getaway on foot to Yorktown, sell the heirlooms, and go by ship to some other city where the Yanceys could never find her.

"So you used Mother's keys to get supplies for your trip—"

"I took only what I needed," Anne said. The slanting flame from the candle made her shadow twist and dance on the bare plastered wall. "And I returned the keys, didn't I? *And* your necklace."

"So you did," Felicity said. "Why'd you return the necklace?"

"It belonged with you," Anne said simply. "You were nice to me, and it seemed as if we might have been friends, if things had been different. I thought you might have already figured out that I'd stolen the necklace from you." She looked Felicity in the eye. "I didn't want you to have a bad impression of me, y'see. I left the necklace where you could find it easily."

"So I would think I'd only lost it," Felicity said, understanding.

A small, sad smile came to Anne's lips. "Giving the necklace back to you made me feel less guilty about keeping your family's heirlooms."

"But you didn't *keep* the heirlooms. You felt so guilty, you put them back too." Felicity got up and moved to the sofa beside Anne. She put a sympathetic hand on Anne's knee. "You're not much of a thief, are you?"

"That's just it. I'm not a thief at *all*," Anne said. "I decided anything would be better than going on stealing for the Yanceys. After I returned your heirlooms, I decided I'd walk to Yorktown and try to find work there. Then came that wretched storm." She stifled a sob. "Thunderstorms frighten the wits out of me, y'see. Ever since Papa died on a stormy night, years ago."

Anne's gaze was fixed beyond Felicity, on some unseen point in the darkness. Felicity had the feeling that Anne was reliving in her memory the night of her father's death. It startled Felicity when Anne suddenly continued. "I went to your window to watch and wait for the storm to let up. But when I pulled back the draperies, I spotted Father Yancey standing across the street, staring at the house, right at *me*. 'Twas like he'd read my mind and knew I meant to try to escape him. Oh, he's the devil, I tell you. The devil himself!" Covering her face with her hands, she burst into tears.

Felicity ached with sympathy for Anne, but she didn't know what to do to help her.

"Father Yancey has everyone fooled, don't you see?" Anne wept through her fingers. "Even my own papa trusted him and thought he was a friend, but all Yancey wanted was the money in Papa's will for taking care of me.

"I don't want to be arrested as a thief and put in jail. But now I suppose I will be. No one will ever believe me over the word of a man like William Yancey!" Anne broke down in huge, racking sobs.

Felicity put an arm around Anne and pulled her close. Anne's thin shoulders shook with her weeping. Felicity seethed with anger at Mr. Yancey for what he'd done to Anne—and to Penny. But now was not the time to voice it.

"Don't worry," Felicity said. "You won't go to jail. Tomorrow we'll tell my father everything. He'll know what to do. He has important friends in Williamsburg who can help you."

Anne lifted hopeful eyes to Felicity. "Really? Would he do that for me?"

"I'm sure of it," Felicity said. "Father's always willing to help someone in need. And tonight you'll stay here and sleep in my bed with me."

14

MERRIMAN FAMILY HEIRLOOMS

Even though Felicity and Anne had so little sleep, they woke up early. They went to the kitchen before Father and Ben were up and prepared breakfast: hominy grits and fried eggs, coffee, biscuits, and buttermilk.

Felicity was amazed at how easy it was to cook with Anne. When Mrs. Hewitt had been there, with her criticism and disapproval, Felicity had felt unsure and nervous in the kitchen. Now, working with Anne, Felicity found that she knew exactly what to do and how to do it. Anne asked for instructions and Felicity gave them with a quiet confidence that even surprised herself.

Anne did exactly as Felicity asked, and the entire breakfast—Father's favorite—turned out perfectly. The grits were smooth and creamy with gobs of yellow butter and just the right amount of salt. The eggs were fried in the cast iron skillet the way Father liked them—soft golden yolk in the center and the whites firm and crispy on the edges. The biscuits were fluffy, the coffee hot, and the buttermilk rich, cool, and sweet.

Father, Ben, and Dawson couldn't have been more pleased when Felicity brought the splendid breakfast in from the kitchen and laid it all out on the sideboard. Father, with a broad smile, told Felicity that Mother would be proud when she heard what a fine cook Felicity had proved to be. Then Felicity told them about Anne, and Anne came into the room.

While everyone ate, Felicity told Anne's story, with Ben and Dawson filling in the parts they knew. Anne sat silently with her shoulders hunched, as if she wanted to make herself as inconspicuous as possible. She barely touched her food.

When Felicity had finished telling Father everything, she asked him if he could help Anne.

"Anne's afraid she'll be arrested as a thief," she explained.

Father put down his fork and turned to Anne. "You have nothing to fear, young lady. It's William Yancey who will go to jail, not you. After breakfast we'll visit my friend Mr. Whythe. There's no better lawyer in Williamsburg, and I'm sure he'll waste no time in bringing charges against Mr. Yancey. Mr. Whythe can also make arrangements to find another guardian for you."

"But none of my inheritance from Papa is left," Anne said, her voice trembling. "And a guardian would have to be paid for my care. Mr. Yancey said I had no other place to go except the poorhouse."

"The parish church often takes on the responsibility of caring for orphans," Father said. "A guardian could be paid from church funds."

"Father, I have an idea," Felicity said. Everyone turned interested eyes toward Felicity. "You know Mother's dressmaker, Mrs. Whitehurst?"

"Of course," said Father.

Felicity ran a finger along the edge of her

drinking glass, unsure what Father would think of her idea. "The last time Mother and I were in her shop, Mrs. Whitehurst mentioned that she wanted to get an apprentice. She needs a girl who's hardworking and easy to get along with and who can sew fast and well.

"Father, that describes Anne." Felicity glanced at Anne, and Anne returned a hopeful gaze. "I was wondering if you might help Anne get a place with Mrs. Whitehurst."

Father steepled his fingers on the linen table-cloth. "Would that be something that would interest you, Anne?"

"Oh, yes," said Anne. "I'd be much happier earning my own keep than depending on other people's charity."

Father smiled. "Then I'll see Mrs. Whitehurst about it this very day. And speaking of appren-tices..." He fixed his eyes on Dawson. "When Publick Times are over, I would be happy to have you stay on, Dawson, as *my* junior apprentice. I could certainly use another one."

Dawson had finished eating, and he pushed

himself back from the table. "The offer is tempting, Mr. Merriman. I've enjoyed working in your store, and it's been a privilege to know all of you and to help Penny. But I miss the adventure of life at sea. I'll work through next week, until Publick Times end, and then I plan to sign on with the first ship sailing out of Yorktown."

Felicity's heart sank. Dawson was going to leave them! "What about Penny?" she asked. "Her sores aren't completely healed yet."

"Penny is much better," Dawson said. "She'll need the salve for only a few more days, and then she'll be good as new."

Father and Ben and Felicity all told Dawson how much they would miss him. But there was one more thing Felicity wanted to say to him. "I never told you how much I appreciate what you did for Penny. I owe you so much and I feel so bad about..." Her eyes darted from Dawson to Ben and back to Dawson. She didn't want Father to know she'd accused Dawson of stealing from him.

"Pshaw," Dawson said. "Everybody makes

mistakes. Even me." He gave Felicity a wink.

Felicity smiled. *Same old Dawson.* She *was* going to miss him. "Seems I've made more than my share of mistakes since Mother has been gone," she said.

Father looked at her in a way that made her think he already knew about her accusing Dawson. "What matters is whether you've learned from your mistakes," he said. "I think your mother will be pleased with the way you've managed things in her absence."

"I feel as if I was stumbling along rather than managing!" Felicity exclaimed.

Father took Felicity's chin and tilted it toward him. "My Lissie, you have done well at handling the responsibilities your mother entrusted to you. Yet she will be most proud, as I am, of the way you've shown a kind and generous spirit to everyone, even under difficult circumstances.

"I suspect you were overwhelmed at times with all you had to do, yet you were eager to help Dawson and Anne and to be kind to Mrs. Hewitt—who, I might add, is much improved.

Her niece tells me Mrs. Hewitt is anxious to have you visit her. It seems she believes you have promise as a cook and wants to give you some of her recipes." Father's eyes twinkled merrily.

Felicity felt a little stunned. She couldn't believe Mrs. Hewitt had praised her. "I'll...go see her today," she managed.

Then Father pushed back his chair. "We have much to do today; we should be getting started. Ben, you and Dawson must open the store, and Anne and I will visit Mr. Whythe and Mrs. Whitehurst. Lissie, what are your plans for the day?"

"I'll do the washing," Felicity announced, "and finish cleaning the house. And," she added, glancing quickly at Anne, "I want to polish Lady Margaret's heirlooms so that they shine like a looking glass." Anne gave Felicity a huge grin.

"'Tis a fine day for cleaning," said Father. He stood up. "And that reminds me. Business at the store has been so brisk during Publick Times, we've done well enough that I won't have to sell Lady Margaret's heirlooms after all. I believe the heirlooms should remain in the Merriman family. Don't you, Lissie?"

"Oh, yes, Father! I do!" Felicity said happily.

Then came the hustle and bustle of everyone getting ready to go out to the day's business. When at last everyone had gone, Felicity was alone again in the stillness of the house. The first few days after Mother had left, the quiet in the empty house had unsettled Felicity, but now it felt peaceful. Sunshine streamed through the tall windows, and floating dust motes shimmered in the light like tiny stars.

It made Felicity think of the heirlooms. How they had gleamed in the sunlight on the day Father unpacked them! The next thing she knew, she was walking into the parlor and over to the heirlooms, almost as if drawn there. The emeralds and silver seemed to glisten even brighter than on that first day.

I wonder, Felicity thought. *I just wonder . . .*

She reached out her hand toward the silver-backed brush. Would she feel the same tingling sensation that she had before? Holding her breath, she lowered her fingers and touched the brush. Nothing happened.

Then, little by little, a strange warmth began to seep into her fingers and up to her hand. The warmth was pleasant and almost . . . friendly.

Was it Lady Margaret's ghost, showing her approval that her heirlooms would stay in the Merriman family?

Perhaps, Felicity thought. *Or perhaps it's only the warmth from the sunlight shining on the silver.*

Did Lady Margaret's ghost even exist?

Felicity looked down at the heirlooms— *the Merriman family heirlooms.* She thought of the Reverend Mr. Ullfers's opinion about ghosts and smiled. She believed she would keep an open mind in the matter, too.

With that, she turned around and went to find the feather duster.

Looking Back

A Peek into the Past

Felicity's mystery takes place during Publick Times, when Virginia's highest court was in session in Williamsburg. There were so many visitors during Publick Times that Williamsburg's population almost doubled overnight. Colonists came to hear the trials in the courts of law and to hear news of the town and the colonies. They also came to learn about the latest clothing, music, amusements, and ideas from Europe.

While court was in session, a fair was held in Market Square, the center of Williamsburg. This was the town *common,* or the place where the townspeople gathered together. During the fair, the square was full of activity. Booths and tents offered all kinds of merchandise. Some booths offered freshly baked tarts and cakes. Others displayed embroidery and merchan-

dise just in from Europe. Farmers from the outskirts of town sold fruits, vegetables, and live chickens and other farm animals.

As people strolled around Market Square, they might see exotic animals, jugglers, acrobats, and puppeteers performing. Fairgoers could listen to fiddlers playing lively music or stop to watch people dancing reels and jigs.

There were all kinds of exciting games, contests, and races to see. Horse races began with the *bang!* of a starting gun, and the cheering crowd could be heard around the track. Another popular contest was trying to catch a pig whose tail was

Horse races were popular events during Publick Times.

lathered with slippery soap! Each night, there were plays and parties. Some of the plays were written by William Shakespeare, England's most famous playwright.

During Publick Times, the taverns were so crowded that they often overflowed. Many men who visited Williamsburg stayed in the taverns, which also served as inns. Visitors went there to talk about business and to catch up on the news.

Everyone was eager for news. The local townspeople chatted with travelers, boatmen, and wagon drivers, who brought news from the towns they had passed through. People also

enjoyed listening to the crew members of sailing ships tell of adventures in faraway places such as Africa, South America, and the West Indies.

Along with all the fun and excitement, however, Publick Times brought danger. Thieves and pickpockets slipped through the crowds and made off with people's valuables. Thieves were not uncommon in Felicity's time, and some really were women and girls.

Modern actors show a colonial thief making off with a stolen pocket watch.

The usual punishment for a person convicted of theft was to be branded on the hand with a hot iron. A person branded with a "T" was marked as a thief for the rest of his or her life. If caught stealing again, a thief would be branded on the other hand or the forehead or would be hanged.

Dishonest people even took advantage of orphans to get rich. Some guardians took in orphans just to get their hands on the children's inheritance or to use the children as workers.

Yet desperate orphans like Anne had only one place to turn for food and shelter—the poorhouse, or *almshouse*. The almshouse gave shelter to the poorest people of the town, but life

Almshouses took in the poorest people, who were forced to work in exchange for basic food and shelter.

there was terribly hard. At many almshouses, overseers forced residents to work and beat them if they misbehaved. People who lived in almshouses had to wear badges everywhere they went, and many townspeople looked down on them. Thomas Jefferson wrote that almshouses were mainly for people who "had no possessions, jobs, or friends."

The luckiest orphans became apprentices, living and working with a master craftsman for many years to learn a trade. Young men in Felicity's time often became apprentices, but girls were rarely apprenticed unless they were orphans. Orphaned girls usually learned a trade such as sewing, weaving, or spinning.

Even though orphans often began apprenticeships at a very young age, they truly were the lucky ones. The skills they gained during their years as apprentices would allow them to earn a good living and a respected place in society.

An apprentice weaver works at her loom.

About the Author

Elizabeth McDavid Jones has lived most of her life in North Carolina. Her earliest passions were animals and writing. As a girl, she especially loved to write stories about animals.

Today, she lives in Virginia with her husband and children. She is the author of two other Felicity mysteries, *Peril at King's Creek* and *Traitor in Williamsburg.*

She also wrote five American Girl History Mysteries: *The Night Flyers,* which won the Edgar Allan Poe Award for Best Children's Mystery; *Secrets on 26th Street; Watcher in the Piney Woods; Mystery on Skull Island;* and *Ghost Light on Graveyard Shoal,* an Agatha Award nominee for Best Children's/Young Adult Mystery.